CW01053096

THE STABBING AT THE SPA

DOG DETECTIVE - A BULLDOG ON THE CASE MYSTERY

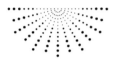

ROSIE SAMS

DOG DETECTIVE - A BULLDOG ON THE CASE

Dog Detective - A Bulldog on the Case

So many of my readers enjoyed meeting Lola Ramsay and Sassy, the Lilac Frenchie, that I knew we had to write more books with these wonderful characters.

You can now grab the first 6 Bulldog on the Case books in one great value box set and also FREE with Kindle Unlimited

Sassy is modeled on Lila, my Lilac French Bulldog. Lila had been returned to her breeder as she was unwanted. At the time, I was looking for an older, small, short-haired dog to rescue. Something I could cuddle, that would keep me company while I was writing. When I met Lila I fell in love with her and that as they say, was that.

Can you believe that anyone would not want her? She is the sweetest little bundle of love you could ever meet. Well, someone's loss was my gain.

Lila is a joy to live with, though she does like to pinch my socks. Nothing makes her happier than getting out of bed and stealing my socks. It has become such a joke that I put a pair on the bed just for this.

Now, all I needed was a new name and so I asked you, my wonderful readers, to come up with a name. There were some great ideas but the one that suited the character the most was Sassy Pants by Sandra H. Thank you, Sandra, we love the name.

I'm so pleased that my wonderful cover designer has managed to bring photos of Lila/Sassy to life for the covers. Much of what Sassy does comes from Lila; you will have to decide if I can hear her talking. I hate to admit it, but I talk to her constantly.

Read on for my next book, where Sassy and Lola are staying in a sleepy British village with a friend. I hope you enjoy it.

Join my newsletter to grab some free short stories

A STAR ENCOUNTER AT CLINTON HALL

"It's just going to be so great." Alice Beecham clapped her hands in delight as she led them up a path between ornamental trees and bushes to the spa that looked like a stately home.

Lola felt her mouth fall open; it was not the purple and orange shell suit that Alice was wearing, or the bright red bag that hung over her shoulder, that caused her to stare. The place was beyond her wildest dreams. It rose out of the greenery like some form of a palace. She couldn't believe that they would be lucky enough to spend the day here. Part of her expected to turn the corner and see one of the royal family, or perhaps an actor out of some period drama, walking toward them.

"The house was finished in 1875, built by London contractors for the Clinton-Smyth's," Alice continued.

Lola could hear Sam Smith and Louisa Meeks whispering behind her. The couple had originally pretended to get together to help foil an evil man. It seemed, to Lola at least, that their relationship had grown into something more. As she watched them her mind drifted back to a man she knew, a love that never had the chance to bloom. A chill ran down her spine and she felt a furry body touch her leg.

"Not bad place," she heard in her mind.

Lola looked down to see Sassy, her lilac French Bulldog smiling up at her. As always, the dog calmed her. Somehow, Sassy was able to send a feeling of love and warmth right into Lola's mind. It pushed away the bad memories and grounded her in the present.

"You shouldn't have gotten her started." Tilly chuckled in Lola's ear and Lola came back to the present. "We will hear every detail about the place before the day is done." Tilly winked to show that she was joking. Though there were at least 20 years between her and Alice and they were very different; still, they were the best of friends.

Behind Tilly, looking perfect as always, was Tanya Buchannan, the woman that Lola was staying with. "Do we have an itinerary?" Tanya asked flicking her perfect blonde bob over her shoulders with a flawlessly manicured nail in baby pink.

Lola ran a hand down her own hair. Though it was long, black, and straight it always seemed to have a mind of its own and even now was flapping around her head like a bin bag in the wind.

"I just thought we would make it up as we go along," Tilly said. "There is plenty to do."

"Will there be socks?"

Lola looked down to see Sassy grinning up at her. Lola raised her eyebrows and shrugged her shoulders remembering not to answer.

"The style is Tudor/Gothic and the cost was £30,000." Alice waited for the gasps. "Yes, a pittance now, but a lot of money in those days," Alice continued.

The whole entourage had ground to a halt.

"Move aside, move aside, this will not do at all," a man's voice, high pitched and grating, carried to them and Lola noticed that Louisa and Sam were almost pushed into the bushes as a tall thin man with ginger hair and a mustache to match barged past with a heavy briefcase in what looked like snake skin in his hands.

Lola blocked his way, bracing herself, and turned to look at Alice. As he pushed into her, she felt him brought to a halt with a humph as the wind was knocked out of him. Her military training came in handy, she would not allow anyone to be rude to her friends.

Sassy let out a Frenchie scream and put herself between the man and Lola. He stepped back so quickly that he ended up stumbling off the path and falling face-first into a bush.

Sassy looked up at Lola. "That showed him."

Lola smiled but wiped it off her face for when he emerged, his face was as red as his hair and he was covered in leaves and debris. It was a shame to see such an expensive, steel grey pinstriped suit dirtied, but Lola couldn't help but raise an eyebrow. "Excuse me," she said and stepped aside.

"You should have more respect," the redhead said and waved his hands at Lola as if to shoo her aside.

"I have plenty of respect... for those who earn it," Lola said and gave him the coldest, hardest stare she could muster. This was not what they wanted out of a relaxing day and she would not let this jumped up... person... spoil her friend's fun.

Sassy put herself in front of Lola once more, squaring her shoulders and growling at him. Though the Frenchie, at this moment, believed she was as ferocious as a trained attack dog, the noises made Lola want to smile. It was so cute.

"Fred, that's enough," a silky woman's voice said and her friends all stepped to the side as an attractive and glamorous woman in her 60s walked toward them. She had red hair, but whereas Fred's was weak, fine, and almost orange, hers was thick, luscious, and like living fire.

Lola knew that she recognized the woman but she couldn't place her and then she heard Alice gasp, her mouth dropping open and all thoughts of the house's history were forgotten.

The woman smiled and walked past them taking Fred with her. Her linen suit was cream, embroidered with gold, and it hugged her body beautifully. The skirt was short for a woman of her age but she had beautiful legs and matching gold sandals. The woman turned and smiled at them, and as she did so, a gold chain appeared from within her suit, the huge diamond on it dazzling them as it caught the light. Then she was gone.

For a moment, Lola wondered if she was a member of the royal family and if she should have curtsied. "Who was that?" she asked, having the urge to reach over and close Alice's mouth.

Tilly shook her head and it was Tanya who answered. "That was Carmine Rivers, the singer."

Lola was none the wiser.

"No socks, she not interesting," Sassy said.

Lola looked down and the little Frenchie's bottom lip jutted out. "No one wearing socks, except Sam and angry man. Why?"

Lola shrugged again, she could hardly tell the Frenchie that it was a warm day and they were going to change into their bathing costumes so there was no point. Besides, such news would only depress Sassy even more, and Lola was not sure how she would cope with the day. A spa was hardly the place for a sock-obsessed Frenchie.

"Alice is a big fan of hers," Tilly continued and Lola pulled her mind away from Sassy. "She will be dying to meet her later, this is so wonderful."

"Tell that to your face," Lola said for Tilly looked decidedly unhappy.

Tilly stepped a little closer so that Alice could not hear. "Carmine has a reputation of being fiery, snobby, and rude. It will break Alice's heart if she is like that to her."

Lola understood and she could see that Alice was still staring after the woman, very star-struck. Lola had a feeling that this would not go well.

RELAXING OR NOT

Lola had never been to a day spa in her life and she had no idea what to expect. As a woman of action, she worried that she would be bored and that the time would drag. It was supposed to be a relaxing day of pampering, but if she couldn't sit still, how would she relax? Luckily, she was in good company but the last thing she wanted to do was spoil it for the rest of them.

The last few months had been exciting, maybe a little too much so for all of them and so Tilly had persuaded them to take this day to relax, recharge, and enjoy. Apparently, Tilly and Alice had visited the spa most years but for the last couple of years, they hadn't managed to take the time.

Here they were, six unlikely friends, seven if you counted Sassy!

The entrance to the spa was magnificent. They walked into a huge foyer that looked like a cave; a waterfall ran down the rocks on each side, misting the air and providing a refreshing feel. They fell into twin pools that spread beneath the glass floor. Magnificent koi in red and white circled lazily beneath their feet. Everyone who hadn't been before gasped, and once more, they blocked the entrance to stare.

Wow, if the rest of the day was even a touch as wonderful as this then they were in for a treat.

After they came through the initial entrance they were in a modern reception where staff members were waiting with big smiles and refreshments. The staff all looked amazing, beautiful, and immaculate in old-fashioned uniforms that matched the house but looked classy. The women and men all wore tuxedo-type uniforms, with crisp white shirts and either knee-length skirts or trousers. Everyone was attractive and their smiles were open and friendly.

Once they were booked in, they were offered a drink from various fruit juices and waters and then shown to the changing rooms. Sam was taken to the men's and the ladies all went through into a luxurious room with changing booths and lockers. It was tiled in a blue and green mosaic and looked both clean and modern as well as soothing and relaxing. There were lots of nooks and crannies and Lola followed everyone else wondering if she would find her way. It meant that each batch of lockers was secluded and although close to the next, they were also private and away from it.

A few other ladies were coming out of the cubicles and putting their belongings into the lockers. Lola unclipped Sassy and the little Frenchie trotted off to explore. Lola could hear her taking great big sniffies as their guide explained the facilities to them.

"There is a fully stocked gymnasium with various exercise classes going on all day. There is everything from HIIT to relaxation and Yoga, just follow the signs to the left of the changing rooms," the guide said.

Lola could see Sassy searching the room, her little tail sticking up like a flag and constantly waving as she sniffed and searched for socks.

"There are a number of treatment rooms in our thermal spa suite where you can relax and unwind..."

"Why no socks?"

"... Feel free to use them as you wish. Bask in the cleansing atmosphere of the herbal caldarium, relax in the rose-infused steam room."

"Oh, I love that one," Alice said clapping her hands in delight.

Sassy had returned to sit in front of Lola, her bottom lip protruding ever so slightly, her eyes wide and sad. Lola reached down and rubbed her ears and then scooped her into her arms. Sassy snuggled against her cheek. "Why no socks?" she asked.

Lola kissed her and tried to listen to the orientation.

"There is the saltwater tranquility pool, the outdoor hot tubs. Feel free to enjoy the grounds and the gardens. You can also book facials, massages, and other treatments with reception."

"Is food included?" Louisa asked.

"It certainly is Miss; breakfast is currently being served in the restaurant. You can eat it there or take a plate to one of the other rooms such as the conservatory or the rooftop terrace."

"I like the sound of that," Tilly said.

"It wasn't open last time we came," Alice said.

"It has only been open a month," their guide added. "Is there anything else I can help you with?"

Lola looked around to see that all of her friends were shaking their heads, she realized that she had been paying more attention to Sassy, rather than the guide, but how hard could it be?

"Have a wonderful day, ladies. Any questions, just ask any member of staff."

"Let's get changed and then grab some breakfast," Tanya said. "I'm with Louisa, I'm starving."

"Me too," Alice said and clapped her hands once more.

"Me Three," Sassy said and licked Lola's cheek. "I like sausage!"

Lola was sure that she would be able to sneak a little sausage for her ever-hungry pal, no one would mind!

"Where are you all going?" Lola asked Tanya.

Tanya flicked her perfect blond bob back over her shoulder and took the leaflet that Lola had been given. "Here, this is your locker number and we are all having lunch at the same time, look, between 1 and 2 pm. Our lockers are all in the same area too."

"I didn't bring a robe or sandals." Lola noticed that all the women who were leaving the changing area were wearing beautiful fluffy white robes and matching sandals. "Alice just said to bring a swimming suit."

As if on cue, Alice opened her big bright red bag and pulled out a robe. It was a fluorescent orange color and Lola knew her mouth dropped open. The robe was bold, audacious and so Alice.

Tanya closed Lola's mouth. "Don't worry, they are provided, all you need is your costume." She waved the papers they had been given and pointed to a number on the top. "Your locker number is like a charge card so you can leave your purse in the locker and pay for any extras when we leave."

Lola shrugged. "Sorry, I must have drifted off."

Tanya chuckled. "I saw you watching Sassy. She keeps you on your toes!"

"Sorry!"

"Don't be." Tanya reached out and touched Lola's arm. "You need to learn to relax. I know you had some awful things happen and I know they still bother you."

Lola kept her face neutral but she was surprised to hear this. She thought she had kept her past away from her friend. Since she had taken on Sassy, the little Frenchie woke her before her nightmares got too bad. Lola didn't think she had woken screaming once in all the time she had been in England. However, it seemed that Tanya was more astute than she gave her credit for. "I'm sorry, I didn't want to bother you."

"It's no bother, but you work so hard. You are always putting the needs of others before your own. At least, for today, just relax and let go."

"I will."

Tanya raised a perfect eyebrow. "I'll believe that if it ever happens!"

Lola chuckled. "Well, at least there shouldn't be a murder."

"Murder, what murder?" Alice asked her face full of excitement.

Tanya shook her head. "You've jinxed it. Now, we're doomed."

SETTLING IN

Sam was ready and waiting for them as they came out of the changing rooms and the party, all dressed in their white robes, except for Alice who had brought her own bright orange one, followed Alice and Tilly to breakfast. They walked down high ceilinged corridors, past a room that housed the swimming pool.

Lola glanced inside. It looked amazing and was laid out like a garden in a hotel. There was the pool and loungers all around it and drifting off into the distance. Exotic plants gave the area a Mediterranean feel and made it seem less like a room and more like it was outside. The ceiling was blue and filled with skylights that let in the sunshine.

People were lounging on the loungers and a few swam or floated in the pool. As they walked, water jets came on and five different waterfalls burst into life causing shrieks of delight from a group of teenage girls. Towards the other side of the pool, Lola could see that it went out into the open air. She couldn't wait to have a swim.

Next, they passed the yoga retreat, a strong smell of lavender drifted out of the darkened entrance and Sassy sneezed. They walked on, everyone chattering excitedly as Lola brought up the back. For a moment, she felt like she was on patrol and her eyes instinctively searched for danger.

"Not bad place," Sassy said and rubbed against her calf as they walked on.

"Thanks," Lola whispered.

Sassy's smile lit up her little face and she trotted ahead, her tail held high and proud.

They passed a group of men and women going in the other direction. They all wore white robes and shoes. Sassy stopped to sniff at their feet. "No socks, what sort of place?"

Lola chuckled, she would have to explain.

"Ohh, that looks like the gym," Louisa said.

"I'm looking forward to a good session," Sam added.

"Not for me," Tilly said. "I have my book and will sit by the pool and just let the world go by. No gossip, no customers, no rushing here and there. It will be wonderful."

"Maybe, a little gossip." Alice grabbed Tilly's arm and the two women chuckled and led the way up some stairs, and into the dining room.

The top of the stairs opened out into a large reception area where breakfast was laid out on huge mahogany tables with everything from a full English to continental. Lots of smaller rooms branched off with tables and chairs spaciously set. White table cloths and gleaning silver cutlery along with a bunch of different flowers on each table gave the rooms a lovely touch. Leading from the dining room was a corridor that led to the conservatory and rooftop terrace.

The robe was luxurious, however, the spa shoes flapped on Lola's feet and she knew they would be no good in a chase. Of course, the idea of the day was that there would be no chases, no fighting, no murders. Lola let out a big sigh and allowed her shoulders to relax.

"I smell sausage, bacon, eggs, muffins, yummy yummy in my tummy," Sassy said, then she sneezed. "Uck, wheat-grass." She wrinkled her tiny nose.

Lola chuckled. "Come on, let's get this breakfast."

"Just help yourselves," Tilly said and wandered over to an area that had cereal and toast.

Lola made for the pans and served herself 3 sausages, 3 bacon, a big spoon of scrambled eggs, and some mush-rooms and tomatoes. On a second plate, she added toast, butter, and marmalade. There was orange and apple juice and water both sparkling and plain. She grabbed a glass of orange and a bottle of sparkling water. Next, she got coffee and saw that everyone was waiting for her. Their trays were considerably less loaded than hers.

"Sorry, I didn't mean to keep you waiting."

"You get me sausage?" Sassy was dancing around in front of Lola, almost tripping her.

"Yes, out my way, little one."

Alice laughed. "I love how you talk to her. It's as if she understands, it's so cute."

Lola shrugged and Sassy spun in a circle and let out a moan; to Lola it said, *of course, I understand.*

"Lead on," Lola said.

"Tables." Tilly pointed to the tables spread around the room, many of which were full of people. "Or we can sit in one of the rooms?" Her arm pointed again to smaller rooms set off the main one. "Or go to the conservatory or the rooftop terrace, both are this way."

"The rooftop terrace," Alice said bouncing on her feet and almost spilling the milk from her cereal.

"I'm happy with that," Tanya said and the others all nodded and mumbled their agreement.

Tilly led them down the corridor and through a door into a huge conservatory that was on the second floor of the building. It was filled with soft chairs, sofas, and coffee tables; many people were eating or lounging in the sun. It had spectacular views of the gardens and Lola's eyes were caught by some huge trees to one side. Could they be?

"This way," Tilly called and Lola forgot the trees as they walked through the conservatory and out a set of double doors. Once more the views were spectacular, the gardens before them in all their green glory. The Queen's Jubilee had been held earlier this year and there was Union Jack bunting in the trees close to the building. Lola smiled as she remembered the celebrations and how Sassy had saved the day.

Behind the bunting, roses, clematis, and flowers of all colors put on a glorious display and there were lots of other plants that Lola didn't recognize but could certainly enjoy.

To one side was a Japanese Zen garden with its clean lines of gravel and statues. Pride of place in the center of the garden, a koi pond was surrounded by Japanese Acer trees with leaves of yellow and bronze, and the living jewels swam in the crystal waters.

"Come," Alice called and Lola looked up to see that her friends had found a table close to the edge and were all sitting ready to eat. "You can enjoy the view later."

Lola joined them at the table and her stomach rumbled.

"Looks like someone's hungry," Louisa said. "Me too, let's eat."

The table buzzed with conversation as they unloaded their trays and then silence fell as they tucked into the abundance of food. Lola felt Sassy pawing gently at her leg. "No forget my sausage."

Lola cut a small piece off and handed it down as surreptitiously as she could.

The table erupted into laughter and Lola looked up guiltily.

"I win," Sam said. "I bet less than a minute."

"I was close," Alice said. "A minute to 2 minutes."

"I had no chance." Louisa chuckled, "I went with within 10 minutes."

"Well, it is within 10 minutes," Sam said and touched her hand. "I think we can share the glory."

Lola chuckled. "Am I that obvious?"

"Yes," echoed around the table.

"More sausage," Sassy said but as she reached down to give her it, Lola noticed that a man was staring at her. A shiver ran down her spine and she moved her eyes away, surreptitiously peeking through her long black ponytail so she could see what he was up to.

WATCHING LOLA

Lola's heart was pounding but her hand was steady, as she reached for her gun! Of course, it wasn't there. She was no longer in the military; also, she was in England so why was the man staring at her with such intensity?

"Not bad place," Sassy said. "Well, if you forget no socks."

Lola looked down to see Sassy leaning against her leg. She stroked the Frenchie on the top of the head and looked back at the man who was eating now and no longer seemed to be interested in her.

Lola studied him closely without looking directly at him. The man was handsome, around her age or maybe a little older than her with tawny brown hair cut short around the sides. There was something military about his demeanor. Lola felt her chest tighten; was he a hitman?

Sassy scratched her leg. "Not bad, sausage."

Lola shook herself, of course, he wasn't! What was wrong with her? Maybe the man was a veteran, that didn't mean he was here for her. Why would anyone be after her? Passing a bit of sausage down, she smiled at the giggles that went around the table and pulled her mind back to the conversation.

"What do you think Carmine Rivers is doing here?" Alice asked, her cheeks were flushed so bright they clashed with her robe.

"Maybe she's just relaxing like the rest of us," Tanya offered.

"I heard she is divorcing," Tilly said. "Someone who knows Jennifer Brown, whose cousin is Jinny Peppers, came into the shop."

"Oh, you know everyone." Alice pouted for a moment but then her face cleared and she took a bite of her cereal crunching on the granola mix for a few moments. "The rumors are that her divorce is coming to a head and that it's going to be expensive for her. There is also a rumor that her ex-husband, Hart Bowers, hit her, and if that is proven, then he will lose a fortune. It was in the music press but never made the mainstream papers."

"I thought he was almost bankrupt," Tanya said as she spread marmalade on her toast without even a single crumb falling onto the pristine table cloth. Lola wondered how she did it. When she took her own plate off the tray, crumbs had gone everywhere.

"Well," Alice's face curled into a conspiratorial smile. "Hart is a movie star, pretty good at it, and invested his money well. I think he is very rich. You are probably thinking about the last boyfriend, Bruce Powell. He was in B movies, he was never good enough for her in my opinion, and he splashed his money around like Henry Cooper and Kevin Keegan in a Brute advert."

"What?" Louisa shook her head as she tried to follow the conversation.

"You know, 'splash it all over,'" Alice tried to do a Henry Cooper impersonation.

Louisa shook her head. "Henry who?"

Groans went around the table.

"Never mind. He spent more than he earned and is now desperate to get a movie role," Alice said. "It's so sad, how could anyone not love Carmine?"

"I don't know," Tilly said. "I heard she was quite a diva and was really hard to work with... not that she's done much in years. How much money can there be left?"

"There has to be loads." Alice's eyes were wide. "All her hits... and they still sell."

"What hits?" Louisa asked and Sam shook his head and shrugged his shoulders.

"I bet you don't know any." Louisa playfully punched Sam's shoulder.

"Sausage," Sassy said.

Lola handed down a bit more sausage and was pretty sure that she got away with it this time. The group was too interested in the conversation about Carmine.

"There was "Shoo Wop and Shoop Shoop," Alice said. "Then, Happy in the Sunshine, which, is one of my favorites. And who could forget, Don't Let Your Man Leave Town?"

"Okay." Louisa held up her hands. "I haven't heard of any of these.

"The youth of today." Alice shook her head and then her eyes turned on Lola.

"I don't know them either." Lola held up her hands in surrender and chuckled. "There wasn't a lot of choice of radio stations out with the guys in Afghanistan."

"No, not that." Alice reached across the table and tapped her hand. "You have an admirer." Alice moved her eyes back to the man who had been looking at Lola earlier.

Lola felt her blood chill as she turned to see that the man had indeed been looking at her. Caught in the act, he quickly turned away.

Was that it? Did he find her attractive? Lola had not thought about a man in quite some time and she was not sure that this was what was happening... but then, maybe it was more logical than a hitman? Even so, she was not interested.

"He's cute," Louisa said.

"He might be, but I don't like rude men who stare." Lola knew she had snapped and her friends all looked down at the table for a few moments. Hopefully, that would be enough to end the conversation.

"Now, back to Carmine," Lola said. "Tell me all about her."

Alice had forgotten the admirer as her face lit up with joy.

AN EX IN THE GARDEN

"More sausage."

Lola looked down to see Sassy staring up at her with such sad eyes that she reached for her plate but it was empty. Shrugging, she wanted to tell Sassy that if she ate much more she wouldn't be able to move, but the little dog seemed to have a never-ending stomach and she never put on weight.

Lola had been like that when she was in the military. She was always too slim and could never put on weight no matter how much she ate. Her friends put it down to the fact that she never sat still. Since she had moved to Great Britain, she had slowed down a lot and she had put on a little weight. She felt better like this and knew that Tilly's baking had a lot to do with it. She chuckled;

when she made the trip here she never expected to make such good friends so quickly. It was nice.

Alice was still regaling them with facts about Carmine and her soap opera lifestyle when Lola watched Alice's mouth drop open. "Is that Bruce Powell?" she asked.

Everyone got up and followed her eyes. She was looking over the railing to the Zen Garden below where a man was looking decidedly unZen.

He paced back and forward kicking up the gravel. It was hard to make out too much from this angle but he had thick black hair and was deeply tanned. He looked around 6 feet tall and had an athletic body. He was wearing the normal robe that everyone seemed to be in.

Alice let out a gasp as a door opened and a flurry of red hair followed by a voluptuous cream robe floated into the garden.

"That's Carmine," Alice squeaked. "Well, I never, what are they doing together?"

"Who is he?" Lola asked.

"Honestly!" Alice had her hands on her hips but then she chuckled. "I should have known you weren't listening. Always investigating some crime."

Lola blushed; she had been listening to Sassy, but she shrugged an apology.

"Bruce Powell is Carmine's last ex. He's an action movie star, I believe he also runs a not-too-successful actor recruitment agency. They dated for a couple of years and some believe he left her, some say it was the other way around. I think she had to have left him; who would leave Carmine?"

Tilly harrumphed.

"Oh, stop it," Alice said, "she's not that bad."

"She can be a bit of a... well, a female dog," Tilly said.

Louisa laughed and Sam's mouth opened a little and closed, he looked just like a fish.

"The new man," Alice said, "is much younger, around thirty I believe and I don't know much about him other than she met him when she was touring a disaster site in some country with earthquakes. He works search and rescue, and he looks so nice. He must be nice to do such a wonderful thing."

"Ah, a hero," Tilly said. "All the women love a hero."

Lola chuckled and remembered her own hero, it was hard for other men to match up to him.

"What are they doing?" Alice asked as she was leaned over the balcony trying to hear what was going on.

"Alice," Tilly shrieked and grabbed ahold of the orange robe yanking Alice's feet back to the floor.

"I wasn't going to fall, I was just...."

"Being nosy." Tilly let out a big breath and put a hand over her heart. "You will be the death of me."

"Listen." Alice was keeping her feet on the floor but was still leaning over and straining to hear.

Though, only the vague sound of angry voices reached them. From Lola's point of view, Bruce was not too happy to see Carmine and was trying to move away. Carmine, on the other hand, wanted to give him a piece of her mind and was following him wagging her finger.

Bruce stopped and turned on her, shoving her hard. Lola was on her feet looking for the easiest way to get down there. Bruce leaned in close to Carmine's face and said something before shoving her again and then he turned and was gone.

"Well," Alice was outraged. "I'm pleased she got rid of him, do you think we should go and see if she is all right?"

Before anyone could answer Carmine went back inside and was gone.

"I will tell her I was a witness... if we see her later. No one should have to put up with that."

"Alice, I think we should give her some privacy," Tilly said.

"Yes, of course." Alice sat back down and looked a little subdued.

"I think I'll get another coffee, anyone want anything?" Lola asked.

"I'll come with you." Alice was on her feet a big smile on her face. "I would love another orange and may have some fruit or more toast. Anyone else?"

A chorus of 'no's' and 'we're good' went around the table.

"More sausage," Sassy said as she trotted along at Lola's side.

"I don't think so," Lola said.

"Don't think what?" Alice asked.

Lola colored. "Sorry, I was trying to decide if I should have anything else to eat." She shrugged.

Alice laughed. "I do that sometimes, hold conversations with myself. I think it's the result of living alone all this time. You can always pretend you're talking to Sassy."

"I might just do that," Lola said as Alice grabbed ahold of her arm and the two of them made it through to the breakfast tables. Lola noticed that the man who had been watching her was following them. She would be ready for him, no matter what he was up to.

NOT INTERESTED

"I guess you think I'm silly admiring a singer as I do?" Alice said as they wandered around the heavily laden breakfast tables.

Everything still looked so fresh and tempting and Lola wondered for a moment whether to have a croissant and some jelly, no, she must call it jam, now she was here in England.

"No, of course, I don't. We all have people that we admire."

Alice laughed a little. "I doubt you do."

"Don't be silly. I admire you and Tilly, I admire Sam for how well he has done, and Louisa. See, I admire everyone."

Alice chuckled some more. "You are so nice to us all."

"On the contrary, you have been so nice to me."

"I love orange juice, do you want anymore?"

"No, thanks, a coffee and a couple of sausages will do me fine."

"Yummy, yummy, yummy, lovey love love you," Lola heard and felt a sensation of being enveloped in love.

Leaving Alice to fill up her glass, she grabbed a bowl and put in two small chipolata sausages and then topped up her coffee.

"That's a strange breakfast." It was the man who had been staring at her.

"Hi, I'm Lincoln, Linc if you prefer." He held out a hand.

"Very funny," she said and turned away from him.

"What's funny?" he asked, blocking her path with such an agile move that she was sure he was a military man.

"That's where I'm staying."

He chuckled and it was a nice sound, his face crinkled forming dimples in his cheeks and it took 10 years off his age. "It's also a nickname, let's try this again." He held out his hand. "I'm Martin, also known as, Lincoln or Linc Hall, I'm pleased to meet you."

"I'm," she smiled and noticed a relaxation around his eyes as he thought his charm had worked, "not interested." Lola turned, dipped past him, and walked away only to turn back when she heard Sassy bark.

The traitorous Frenchie sat in front of Lincoln getting her ears rubbed and looking mighty pleased about it, too.

"He nice," Sassy said as Lola made her way back. It had been such a perfect put-down that she was annoyed to have to crawl back to collect her dog.

"I love your dog," Linc said, still bending down to rub Sassy's ears.

The Frenchie had her tiny pink tongue peeking out from her purple lips and was making grunty groany noises of sheer joy.

"What's her name?"

Sassy woofed that she was Sassy and Lola almost chuckled. The little dog was so sure she had found a new friend that it would be hard to get her to leave. For a moment, Lola was going to say she's called, come back and you get a sausage, but she sighed. "She's called Sassy."

"Sassy Pants," Sassy woofed, obviously wanting to impress this man with her full name.

"Well, actually, her full name is Sassy Pants."

He chuckled and it made him look even more handsome. "It suits her. How come you get to bring her in?"

It was not an accusation just a comment. Lola realized that she had taken Sassy's service jacket off once they were inside. It was very warm in the spa and she realized that it would only make Sassy hotter. "She's my service dog."

He raised an eyebrow as he stood up. "Really, may I ask..." his words trailed off, and a slight pink tinge spread across his cheeks. "Sorry, it's none of my business. She seems good with people."

"She is," Lola knew her answers were still clipped, almost to the point of being rude. Did this guy deserve that?

"I have a friend who just got a German Shepard to help with his PTSD. It looks a mean thing but is really sweet and it has helped him out no end. It's not as sweet as this one though." He bent down and scooped Sassy into his arms rubbing her against his cheek.

"Stubble spiky and tickles." Sassy licked his cheek.

The door into the restaurant area was pushed open with force and the cream robe and red hair of Carmine swept into the room. Up close you could see that the robe had a matching fur trim at the cuffs and collar and Carmine was heavily made up with bright evening red adorning her tight lips. The chain hung around her neck but the diamond was out of sight.

Trotting behind her, balancing a box with a dozen or so files, a Chanel drink bottle, and a large Chanel bag, was an average-looking blonde woman, with a face that spoke of stress and exhaustion. This had to be Jinny Peppers, the assistant. Jinny looked to be in her forties, but she could be older. It was hard to tell as her face was screwed up tight with stress.

Carmine's face was tight, the tightness that comes from barely controlled anger. Though she flounced about as if the world was roses and unicorns, her body was, in fact, stiff and full of rage.

Lola had taken her eyes off Linc and Sassy and they were pulled to Alice. "Oh, no," she mumbled.

Alice had a big adoring smile on her face as she rushed to intercept Carmine. "Miss Rivers, it is so good to meet you. I'm so happy, so overwhelmed. I saw what happened in the Zen Garden. I will be your witness. I will tell everyone how awful he treated you."

Carmine turned in slow motion, but even so, Jinny had to jump to get out of her way and she dropped a file. The look on her face was one of horror.

Jinny scooped down to retrieve it and then ran around so that she was behind Carmine once more.

"Did I ask for your interference?" Carmine barked at Alice, her eyes scanning her up and down and her face curling into a scowl. "You are the reason I can rarely go anywhere, people," the word was said as if it soiled her tongue, "People are like flies. They crowd all around me, buzzing and pooping out their opinions."

Lola stepped forward, but a hand on her shoulder held her back.

"Not now," Linc said. "I will deal with this." He handed Sassy back to Lola and followed Carmine along the corridor.

FLIES SETTLE ON

Lola put Sassy down without dropping her tray and walked across to Alice. The look of shock was still etched onto her face.

"She's obviously upset," Alice said. "Still hurting and angry at Bruce, it was silly to approach her at this time."

Lola wanted to say that Carmine was the silly and rude one, but she knew that wouldn't help. Sassy was cuddling up to Alice's legs and offering her support. Maybe, that was all that was needed.

"Look at you, hungry I guess," Alice said and she walked over to the English breakfast section and grabbed a bowl and a sausage. "Come on, lots to do."

Lola smiled, Alice was resilient and even though this had hurt her, she would not let it get her down and spoil the rest of the day.

They walked through the conservatory, Sassy taking her job of consoling Alice even more seriously now that a sausage was on offer. Once out on the rooftop terrace, Lola noticed that Carmine had taken a table not far from theirs and that Linc was making eyes at her. The man was attractive and Carmine was interested. Lola felt a flush of anger and then realized how ridiculous it was. After all, she was not interested in him, but somehow, this confirmed her reason for keeping men at bay. *Really!* Her mind said but she pushed the voice away.

As she walked, she saw Carmine gesture for Linc to join her. The man put on a big smile and sauntered across. Lola shook her head but took a route that passed as close to Carmine's table as she could without being obvious.

As she got closer she pushed her napkin off the tray, it fluttered to the floor and she bent down to retrieve it.

Linc was at the table, smiling at Carmine and the star was definitely interested. Lola bit her lip for a moment and then stood up.

"What's your name, handsome?" Carmine purred. "Come sit here." She patted the seat next to her, the sunlight really showed her age despite the heavy makeup and the obvious Botox in her cheeks.

"Some people call me Fly," Linc said, his voice was deeper, more sultry, and he chuckled. "But then again, flies settle on poop, maybe that's why you attract so many." With that, he turned and walked away. As he passed he gave Lola a wink.

Carmine's face dropped, and her eyes widened but she recovered quickly. "Jinny, fetch me champagne and make it a good one."

Lola returned to their table to find Sassy on Alice's knee eating little bits of sausage.

"I cheered her up good," Sassy said.

"Hmmm," Lola mumbled.

"What was that all about?" Tilly asked.

"Carmine got her comeuppance."

"I never did like her," Tilly whispered.

"What plans do we have for the day?" Louisa asked.

Lola noticed that Alice's eyes drifted across to Carmine but then she hugged Sassy a little tighter and put a smile on her face. "What we normally do is have an hour or so here, enjoying breakfast, and then around 9 am, we go and have a swim and then spend some time by the pool reading or go in the spa or the various treatment rooms. There is sea salt, rose infusion, and a sauna, then we sit by the pool to dry and then go for a walk before lunch."

"We thought we would go to the gym after we leave here," Louisa said and Sam nodded his agreement.

"Don't go too soon." Alice was shaking her head. "You need to digest first and we all need to hear about you two and about Sam and how you are getting on in the Police Force."

Sam and Louisa both cleared their throats and lowered their now red-looking faces.

"You can't hide it," Tanya said. "It's obvious the two of you are more than just friends."

Sam took Louisa's hand. "I guess we are, but we are still the best of friends."

Louisa chuckled. "It was such a good move to pretend to be together. If we hadn't done this... I don't think he would have ever asked me out and yet we have so much in common."

"Your admirer appears to be back now he's been rebuffed, but I would avoid such a fickle man," Alice said tapping Lola's hand.

"Linc was all right," Lola said.

"But he went from you to Carmine." Alice pulled her bright orange robe tighter around her as if such a betrayal chilled her to the bone.

"No, he gave Carmine a piece of his mind for being so rude."

Alice's mouth dropped open and a smile came over her face. "Oh, I don't think he should have done that... he might get into trouble and she is very influential."

"I think he can look after himself," Lola said. "Now, what are our plans?"

"I'm going to a yoga class at 11 and then for a facial before lunch," Tanya said. "There are still places if anyone wants to join me."

Lola shook her head and turned her eyes to Tilly and then Alice.

"We were going..."

The sound of the Shoo Wop and Shoop Shoop song blared out from a phone behind them and all eyes turned to Carmine. The phone was on one of the glass coffee tables vibrating annoyingly. The glass made the song even more grating than it was and Lola realized that she had heard it before.

Sassy let out a low whine.

Lola could see Jinny hovering in her seat, her bottom just off the chair as she leaned forward not knowing whether to answer the phone or not.

"Leave it," Carmine barked.

After a few more cycles through the most annoying part of the song, the phone was silent.

"Footbath!" Carmine barked and Jinny jumped up from her seat dropping another folder before running off the terrace.

"What was that all about?" Louisa asked.

They all shook their heads but Lola could see that Carmine was upset, something was going on here.

A BLISSFUL FOOTBATH

The friends continued to talk. Sam brought them up to speed on his training to become a police constable. It was going well, and the pride in his eyes almost brought tears to Lola's. The young man had come so far from the scared boy who was mean to fit in with the crowd.

"Angry man," Sassy said.

Lola followed Sassy's gaze to see the ginger-headed man who had been so rude to them earlier. He was still dressed in his suit and carrying the briefcase. As he sat down the phone started ringing again. The noise grated on Lola's nerves and she hoped that Carmine would answer it this time.

While sipping at her coffee, Lola kept her eye on the star. The man had a big bundle of paper that he was spreading out over the coffee table. He pushed the phone to one side and it was clear that he was not happy with who was calling.

"Will she answer that?" Sam asked.

"Just let it go," Louisa took his hand.

"It's my favorite tune, I might see if I can get it for my own phone," Alice said and she was bopping away to the music in her seat, her eyes closed.

"No," went around the table and they all chuckled. It lightened the mood; after all, they were here to relax.

"Let me tell you more about the house's history," Alice said and Lola put her mind back on the meeting going on to her left.

"Won't he sign the papers yet?" the ginger man said.

"Oh, just leave it, Fred, what did you want today?"

"We need a stunt to get sales moving again, remember. Here are a few ideas." He pushed a list across the table.

Lola could see that he was not happy and the way his voice carried told her he didn't care who knew.

The phone started again as Carmine picked up the piece of paper.

Alice was bopping to the music on the phone while the rest of them wanted to cover their ears and take a hammer to it.

It Shooped and wopped and shoop shooped for what seemed like forever. Once it stopped Carmine looked at the list, her face pulled even tighter and her red lips were like two thin lines of blood. "These would make me look like a fool. Why did I hire you, if you are coming up with such rubbish?"

Lola could only just make out what they were saying. "Who is that with Carmine?" she asked, suddenly feeling the need to know more.

"That is Fred Stilby, her new manager," Alice said. "Her managers have never been very good, I wish she would find someone better, someone who can get her music back where it belongs."

The phone started again, vibrating across the glass table as if it was dancing to the annoying and grating tune.

"Oh, please," Tanya said and flicked her blonde bob over her shoulders.

Alice stopped her bopping and looked a little embarrassed.

"Ah, at last!" Carmine shrieked causing them all to turn and see Jinny coming back in carrying a rather large foot-bath that was sloshing water as she put it down. Kneeling at Carmine's feet she set it up and then picked up each of Carmine's feet, removing a slipper that matched her robe complete with fur and placed each foot in the water.

Lola noticed that Fred curled up his nose a little when Carmine was not looking. He didn't care for, or respect the star, she was simply a payday.

For the next twenty minutes, they tried to relax and talk but it was constantly interrupted by the shrilling of the Shoo Wop and Shoop Shoop song.

"Just answer it or turn it off," Fred said a little too loudly. "But don't you go let him creep back in."

Carmine turned her eyes on him and he shrank away from her. "You should be careful."

Lola noticed Sassy darting across the roof between them. The little Frenchie jumped onto the glass table slipping a little. She spun and picked up the phone without missing a beat. It continued to Shoo Wop as she trotted back across the table as proud as punch. Taking one look at the astonished Carmine, Sassy dropped the shooping phone in the footbath before galloping back to them.

The noise died down to a gurgle.

Sassy was chuckling to herself as she jumped onto Lola's knee and curled up there.

A flurry of gasps went around their table before they carried on talking.

"Let me tell you more about the house and the local area," Alice said.

Lola bit back her own chuckle; what would Carmine do? Right now her face was red and her fists were clenched, would she make a scene?

A shriek from Carmine cut through the air.

"Oh, oh," Sassy said and covered her ears with her paws.

HISTORY

Carmine jumped to her feet and scrabbled about in the footbath until she found her phone. "Jinny," she called, shaking the phone at the quivering assistant. "Do something!"

Jinny took the phone and looked at Fred. He shrugged and gathered up his paperwork. "Just take it easy, Carmine," he said.

Carmine leaned over him. "I can fire you too," she said, and ignoring him, she stormed across the rooftop. "Where is that rat?"

Lola started to stand but before she could Linc had stepped in between her and Carmine. He gave the woman a hard stare and blocked her way.

"Let me go, you oaf," she shrieked. "I will skin that rat for what it did."

Linc stepped in front of her each time she tried to dart around him. His movements were calm and controlled. Thwarted, she beat her hands against his chest and then turned and fled from the roof crying.

Fred had picked up his papers and his briefcase. "I don't earn enough for this!" Shaking his head he walked out.

Lola turned back to the table her friends all had their mouths open and their eyes wide.

"Relaxing place this," Lola said and they all burst out laughing.

Lola threw Lincoln a smile, he touched an imaginary cap and went back to his table. It looked like he was prepared to save her, but his chasing her days were over. Lola felt a little disappointed but she shook it off. This was silly, she hadn't been interested.

"Let's talk about the house," Alice said. "The very conservatory we walked through, well, not that one, there's a funny story about that. The original conservatory once housed 2000 plants. The owners brought exotic plants back from all over the world. It was, however, accidentally destroyed. In 1942, a Lancaster bomber exploded on a nearby runway, and pieces of the plane destroyed the conservatory."

"Was it always a home?" Louisa asked.

"No, goodness gracious, no. In fact, it has spent more time empty than occupied. Isn't that a little sad?"

Nods and murmurs of agreement went around the table.

"Is it safe yet?" Sassy whispered from beneath her paws.

"She's gone," Lola whispered.

"Phew, I live dangerously but the mission had to be completed."

Lola chuckled and then pulled her mind back to the conversation as Tanya was staring at her.

"The house has been a home to the Clinton-Smythe's until 1903. Since then, it has been the offices of the following; an electric company, the British Beet Corporation, and a Morris Garages car dealership. It has also been used as a turkey farm, a cattery, and kennels, as an electronics and communications research center, as a French restaurant, and wait for it..." Alice paused for dramatic effect.

Everyone made sure they were giving her their full attention.

"I hope this doesn't put you off your day," Alice said. "It was used as a maggot breeding factory."

"A what?" Louisa asked.

"Oh, dear, I knew I should have stopped her," Tilly said.

"For breeding maggots... for fishing, I presume," Alice said with a big smile on her face.

"How on earth do you breed maggots?" Louisa asked looking a little green around the gills.

"I think on that note we should take a little walk," Lola said, it was not something she wanted to think of while she was trying to relax.

Alice, on the other hand, had a big grin on her face. "History is so fascinating."

"Tell us more about the Clinton-Smythe's?" Tilly said and winked at Lola.

That was all she needed, Alice was in heaven as she told them about all the generations of the family and how they eventually died out in 1903. It was a little sad, a once-promising family had disappeared. They were now nothing but a footnote in history.

"Let's take a walk," Tanya said. "I want to see a bit more of the place."

"We're going to the gym," Louisa said, "We will see you back up here at lunch."

"Have fun," Alice said as they got up and walked away.

"Young love," Alice said and stared after them with misty eyes.

The rest of the friends made their way down the stairs and were walking along a corridor that connected two parts of the building when Alice let out a gasp. "That's Hart Bowers."

"Who?" Lola asked as she looked at the man walking towards them. He was tall and good-looking with salt and pepper hair and an impressive frame beneath the white robe.

"Carmine's soon-to-be ex-husband. What is he doing here?"

"I think we should keep out of it," Tanya said. "I fancy a swim."

"Yes, yes, of course, this way." Alice lead them along the corridor and opened a door into the pool area. It was so warm that it was like walking into a tropical paradise.

Lola watched for one more moment as Hart stormed away from them.

"Man angry," Sassy said.

"I can see he is."

"Did you say something?" Tilly asked.

Lola colored a little. "I was just saying, he looks angry, I guess Carmine has a way with people."

Tilly chuckled. "She sure does."

As they joined their friends at some loungers, Lola couldn't help but wonder what Hart was doing here?

Alice had given them plenty of history on the house, maybe she should get some history on this marriage?

TOO HEAVY

The ladies claimed some loungers and left their robes and bags on them before wandering over to the pool.

"This is a saltwater swimming pool," Alice was still telling them about the building but Lola couldn't help but notice that Sassy was sad.

"What is it my little munchkin?" she asked picking her up.

"No socks and where you going?"

"For a swim. You will be fine, just wait here."

Lola kissed her between the ears and put her down. Sassy rocked back onto her butt sticking her back legs out in front of her. Her bottom lip was protruding and she looked most unhappy.

"You will be fine, sit on the lounger for a few moments," Lola said.

Tanya walked past her and stepped down into the pool. She was wearing a swimsuit covered in exotic flowers; it really suited her and looked so feminine. Lola was wearing a black speedo swimming suit that was simply plain and functional, but suddenly, she didn't want Linc to see her.

"I love how you talk to that dog," Tanya said as she stepped into the pool.

Alice was wearing a purple and orange striped costume and Tilly had on a plain green one that was pretty and had a small skirt around her waist.

Lola followed them into the pool just as the water jets came on. There were five lots of jets in total.

Alice let out a whoop of joy and swam to one end where a circular area was bubbling like a jacuzzi with one wall full of water jets that sprayed down onto the water. Alice swam straight into the area and was tossed about by the water. She was laughing out loud.

Sassy jumped up and raced around to where Alice was, the little Frenchie was barking her head off. She ran along the edge of the circle trying to reach down and grab Alice.

Lola whistled. "Sassy!" The Frenchie either couldn't hear or was too worried to listen. Lola swam over and into the circle of wild water. She could understand why Alice was laughing so much. The air beneath her was powerful and lifted her up and tossed her about sometimes putting her under the jets around the side. Lola swam against it and popped her head up through the jets just in front of Sassy.

Sassy peddled backward her eyes bulging. "Oh, my, I thought you was a gonna!" She flopped down onto the tiles, panting hard. "Did you save Alice?"

"Alice is fine, she is having fun, this is not dangerous."

Sassy shook her head as if to clear water or clear the strange idea that this wasn't dangerous from her head.

"Looks dangerous."

"No, we're fine, you can relax, I will look after everyone in the water."

Sassy sat down again. "Hmmm, not sure about that."

"Maybe you could look for some socks?"

For a moment, Sassy's eyes lit up but then they faded again. "No socks here, I don't like this place."

"Don't be sad, I will get you some more food soon and it's only for today."

Sassy lay down at the side of the pool, her head on her paws. "Be careful, bad water smells wrong."

"I will don't you worry." Lola left her little dog to join her friends.

"That was fun," Alice said. "I do love this pool."

"I'm going to do some laps before the jets start again," Tanya said.

"We should all do some," Tilly agreed.

Lola began to swim laps with her friends up and down the pool. Sassy was running alongside barking once more.

"Too heavy, too heavy," Sassy shouted.

Lola swam over. "What do you mean?"

"I can't save you if you sink, you're too heavy!"

"Are you trying to say I'm fat?"

"Just too heavy," Sassy said.

"Look, Sassy Pants, everything is all right, you go and sit with my robe and protect it. I've heard that sometimes bad people take them, can you manage that?"

Sassy bared her teeth and growled. "I sink my teethies into any thieves. I save all robes, you bob about in the water like heavy things."

Before Lola could say anything else Sassy had trotted back to the loungers. She lay on top of Lola's robe her eyes vigilant in case anyone should try to sneak up on her.

As Lola returned to her swimming she noticed that Carmine was in the corner with Jinny. The assistant had a large hunting knife and was showing it to Carmine. Whatever was happening now?"

THE BOYFRIEND

For the next twenty minutes they swam in the pool and it was glorious. Just the right temperature, the salt instead of chlorine making it feel like being in the sea. However, Lola kept one eye on Sassy. The Frenchie had fallen asleep on her robe, her guarding duties forgotten. Sassy loved the heat and always found the warmest spot to laze in. The high ambient temperature of the room would be heaven for her if she would just relax. Seeing her finally sleeping was a lovely sight and Lola felt her heart melt a little.

Every time the bell went off, to warn them that the water jets were coming on, Alice swam to the next lot of jets. They had only one left. It was a large waterfall that came out of a stainless steel flute. It was about 2 feet wide and looked powerful and a lot of fun.

Lola was amazed at Alice's energy and delight in everything. The rest of them were having trouble keeping up.

Lola came to the end of the pool, she swam under and into a roll and then pushed off the wall as she came out. Once more she was heading down the pool to pass where Carmine and Jinny were sitting. On the last pass, Carmine had been shaking her head at Jinny. It was something to do with the knife and Lola was curious. Why did the singer and her assistant have such a lethal-looking weapon? It was totally out of place in the relaxing spa. It didn't fit in with the two ladies' characters, either, and Lola's mind hated an unsolved mystery.

As Lola drew nearer she could see that Jinny was sitting almost at Carmine's feet reading from a laptop. The knife was nowhere to be seen. What had happened to it?

Lola turned again and swam back to the other end of the pool. She was catching up with Alice and Tilly. The two ladies were chatting as they swam. Glancing around she saw that Tanya was taking a breather.

Lola waved but as she did the bell rang again and Alice let out a whoop of joy. Lola found her arm grabbed as Alice and Tilly made their way to the waterfall.

"We have to do them all," Alice said. "It's our tradition."

Lola chuckled as she followed the ladies to the water plume and they all swam under the powerful stream. It was strong and invigorating and they stayed under the pounding water for a few moments laughing and just enjoying being alive. It reminded Lola of quiet times in a combat zone. You learned to enjoy every moment to the full. So often, we take things for granted and let the simple joys pass us by unnoticed. That was not Alice's way and Lola was pleased to be reminded that life was for living and for enjoying.

Swimming through the waterfall they all leaned against the side of the pool and looked out through the stream of water. It was exhilarating. The air was salty and seemed full of ozone. It was fresh and almost like they were out in a storm.

All too quickly the water stopped.

"I think I could manage a cucumber water," Tilly said.

"That would be delightful," Alice agreed.

Lola nodded her agreement and they swam across to Tanya and then all got out of the pool.

Alice and Tilly were leading and as they stepped from the water an attractive man in his late twenties came through the door to walk past them. His hair was sun-kissed brown and styled to perfection, there was just a touch of stubble on his square jaw and the blue eyes could grace a cologne poster. He glanced down at Lola and Tanya, his eyes taking more than a casual interest.

"Ladies, it's very nice to meet you."

Tanya smiled but stepped out and walked past him with nothing but the briefest nod. Lola waited for him to walk past, but instead, he offered her his hand. It was awkward, she was not interested in this man either, but she felt that to refuse would be rude and churlish.

"Thank you," she said as she stepped from the pool. "Now, please excuse me."

"I can't meet up right now." He leaned in close, too close. "But if you give me your number, we could get together sometime."

"No, thanks." Lola walked past him pulling her hand from his. She walked over to the water dispenser where the ladies were pouring cups of the cooled cucumber water. "What is wrong with this place?" Lola asked.

Alice chuckled. "He was just being polite, I'm sure it was nothing more."

"Really! It didn't come across that way."

Alice was shaking her head. "Do you know who that was?"

"No, should I?"

"He's Scott Brussard, he's dating Carmine."

Lola felt her mouth drop open. The man was half Carmine's age and she was sure he had been flirting with her. She also realized that where she climbed from the pool was hidden from Carmine's view. This man was a player and he would take any opportunity to play!

As they walked back to the loungers Lola let her eyes follow Scott as he made his way around the pool to Carmine. When he greeted her it was all kisses and adoration but that had not been the feeling he had given her earlier.

"You wet!" Sassy said.

"Sorry, I just got out of the pool."

Chuckles greeted her and Lola looked up to see that her friends had watched her talk to Sassy. She shrugged and placing a towel over her knee pulling Sassy onto her lap.

"Tell me about him," Lola said to Alice.

"I only know a little. They have been dating for about 4 months. He runs his own IT company and he met her because in his spare time he does search and rescue. Carmine was filming on the moors and he was there in case anything went wrong. The same day, a young girl went missing, Scott headed the search and he brought her home."

"I saw that, but didn't see anything about Carmine."

Alice let out a big sigh. "It was going to be in a documentary but it got canceled. I don't know why. There was a rumor that it would relaunch her career."

"They started dating after that?" Lola asked.

"So I believe."

Sassy had curled up into a little ball and was now snoring. It was a cute sound that always made Lola smile.

"Isn't she hot?" Alice pointed at Sassy.

"She loves the heat, she would curl up in the conservatory all day if I'd let her. Have there been any rumors of him cheating?"

"Who?" Alice's eyes were wide. "Oh, Scott, no, why would he?"

"I don't know, just an instinct."

Lola let Alice return to reading her book and let her eyes wander over to the celebrity across the pool. Carmine was handing something over to Scott. It was a gift, wrapped in gold paper with a golden bow with long tassels. There was something desperate in her eyes as she sat back and watched.

Scott held the gift and a big smile came over his face, then he turned and she could only see his back. Despite this, Lola got the impression that he was playing her. There was something extravagant about his gestures about the way he stood. He reminded her of a peacock displaying all his plumage to attract the peahens.

He opened the gift but Lola couldn't see what it was. She could see, even from this distance, that Carmine had expected something in return. Scott leaned forward and kissed her lips and along her neck mumbling something to her. As he sat down she could see the aging singer was smiling. She leaned against him and Scott put his arm around her.

Lola craned forward trying to see what he had received but it was blocked by the back of another lounger.

Carmine was all smiles and exuberance. Scott, on the other hand, seemed too much like a player to Lola, nothing about him seemed genuine. As he settled back into the seat, Jinny scuttered away, no doubt to fetch refreshments.

Lola lay back to take a few moments. There was no story here, but what had that knife been for? Did Carmine suspect that Scott was cheating? Did she plan to take her revenge? Was that why her face had fallen when he didn't return her gift?

The sound of Tilly's laughter pulled Lola's mind back to her friends. Today was simply for relaxing, there was no need to invent a mystery.

As she closed her eyes Carmine's phone began to ring once more. It looked like Sassy's intervention had not worked.

Sassy woke up. "Really!"

HOT HEADS IN THE HOT HOUSE

Lola closed her eyes and just chilled for a while. The heat after the exercise was so nice and with Sassy curled up on her lap, it was very relaxing.

A little paw tapped on Lola's hand and she opened her eyes. Sassy was looking up at her and tapped her hand again. "Sorry," Lola said and began to stroke the Frenchie's tummy once more. Sassy let out a sigh of contentment and Lola closed her eyes, making sure that she kept stroking.

"Shoo Wop and Shoop Shoop," blared out across the tranquil pool. Lola jerked awake and let out a sigh, she had to do something, but the racket stopped almost immediately.

Lola was hoping that the star had finally turned off her phone and she relaxed back down as did her friends.

"Sorry," Alice said. "I'm sure it's just her fans, it's usually so relaxing here."

"Don't worry," Lola reached across and patted her arm. "We won't let it spoil things. A few more minutes of chill time and then we should do something else."

"Oh, yes, the salt room is my favorite," Alice said. "It would be too hot for Sassy, though."

"I stay here and guardies long chairs," Sassy woofed.

Lola stroked her behind the ears. "She will be fine here."

Relaxing back down Lola thought that 10 minutes might stretch to an hour. It was still morning, there was no rush, and there was something about the atmosphere of the spa that made it easy to relax. Maybe there was some herbal infusion that made them all drowsy — *or maybe you've just been working too hard and it's catching up with you?*

With her eyes closed, she let out a sigh and relaxed a little more. A paw gently moved her hand back to stroking duties. Lola chuckled.

"Why don't you answer your phone!?" A man's voice, angry and frustrated echoed across the room and the friends all jerked back to the present.

Lola's eyes flew open and her legs swung off the lounger. Sassy, disturbed by the sudden movement, clung on and dug her claws into Lola's flesh, luckily the towel helped them both.

Lola looked across the pool to see Hart Bowers standing in front of Carmine. Jinny was bouncing about on her toes behind him, waving her arms and shrieking. Carmine's face was red, her lips drawn tight, and Scott looked a little mystified.

"Jinny, quiet please, I can't think," Carmine said while still lounging in Scott's arms.

Though there was a pool between them, Lola could hear every word. There was something about the tiled room that caused raised voices to travel. No doubt, the designers of the spa had never expected shrieking guests.

"Oh, oh, trouble," Sassy said and jumped back onto the lounger and placed herself between Lola and the melee. Her shoulders were squared, her muscular little body ready for battle and a deep lilac line ran down her back where her hackles were raised.

"Calm it, little one. They can sort this out between themselves," Lola whispered into Sassy's ear, stroking her and pretending to her friends that she was just soothing the dog.

"Nasty lady upset Alice," Sassy barked.

"Easy, girl," Lola said and pulled Sassy to her, once more stroking her tummy. Sassy instantly relaxed and flopped back against Lola to enjoy the attention.

Across the pool, Scott had stood up and put himself between Hart and Carmine. "Not cool, man," he said. "Don't shout or threaten the lady, you hear me?"

The two men were about the same size, Hart was more thickset and carried a little too much weight around his middle. He was, however, still a striking-looking man. Scott was tall and muscular but a little wiry. No doubt from many hours spent walking the moors in his role as search and rescue. His physique also reminded Lola of that of a climber. The man was strong despite his smaller frame.

"I didn't threaten her... and son... that is no lady!"

Carmine let out a huff of disgust and stood. Pushing Scott aside she faced up to her ex. "What do you want?"

"Hey," Scott called but he backed away and shook his head. For a moment, Lola thought that he would just walk out, but he seemed to think better of it and moved closer, as if ready to intervene.

"Just a chat, if you had answered that ridiculous phone I wouldn't have had to resort to this!" Hart spread his arms in front of him and shook his head. "I always hated your dramatic ways, but this time you went too far."

Lola noticed that a few other people were getting up and walking out of the pool area.

"You! You! You have the audacity to say that I went too far!? It's you who's dating a supermodel. A mere girl, half your age and flaunting it in my face." Carmine's cheeks were as red as her hair.

Hart laughed and turned a pointed look at Scott. "She's twenty-four, and I guess toy boy here is your age?"

"Leave him out of it." Carmine beat her fists on Hart's chest.

The older man didn't flinch, it was as if he was used to this.

"Oh, this is awful," Alice said. "Do you think I should..."

"NO!" all the friends said at once.

"Hey, Carmine, love, stop that," Scott said and he pulled her gently away.

Carmine threw herself against Scott's chest, sobbing dramatically. "You see what I have to put up with? It is too much."

"It's all right, let's go somewhere quieter and talk." Scott looked at the other man and Hart nodded.

"I'm not going anywhere with him, you see how aggressive he is," Carmine said. "If I wasn't such a strong woman, I would be afraid."

"Look!" Hart said. "All I want is for you to quit these nasty lies." He stood for a second and then turned as if to go.

"Lies. Oh," her voice was overly dramatic. "She pulled from Scott's arms and turned to face him.

"In fact, give me back my ring." Hart reached towards her.

"It was a gift, it's mine now." She clutched onto the chain at her neck.

Hart reached out as if to take it, then she slapped him across the cheeks. The smack made a resounding crack before Carmine ran from the corner sobbing with an Oscar-winning performance.

Carmine ran around the pool and past them before leaving via the door to the ladies' changing rooms.

"Oh, at last," Tilly said.

Alice looked sad.

"Nasty lady not sad," Sassy said, "but Alice is, I go cuddle, make better."

Jinny stood on the spot for a few more moments and then she turned and fled after her employer.

Scott and Hart were talking, but they had lowered their voices. Lola wanted to hear so she got up and dived into the pool, swimming around until she was close enough to hear.

The two men hadn't spotted her and though there was a little too much testosterone between them there was no real sign of aggression.

"I couldn't let you hit her," Scott said.

"I've never hit her... or any woman," Hart said. He ran a hand through his hair and pointed at some chairs. They were over by the entrance into the hallway. Scott nodded and Lola swam over as they walked across. She was sure that they were too invested in their own problems to take any notice of her.

Once they were sat, Lola hunkered down in the water as close as she dared and leaned against the wall. To all intents and purposes, she was just taking a breather from her swimming.

Though she didn't know why she wanted to hear what they were saying, instinct told her it was important.

At that moment Sassy let out a shriek of despair. Lola looked across the pool to see the little Frenchie staring into the water where she had dived in. Sassy was barking and in such a state that Lola couldn't make out what she was saying.

Lola turned and swam across the pool to see what was wrong. The sound of Sassy's wail filled her with dread.

BUSTED

Lola swam up to Sassy. "What is it?"

Sassy leaped back, her eyes wide and incredulous. The Frenchie let her mouth drop open and she ran and jumped at Lola. As she was flying through the air, Lola kicked back. Sassy was going to sail straight over her and land in the pool. Though some Frenchie's could swim, not all could, and such a leap would plunge the little pup deep into the water.

As she was over the top of Lola, Sassy realized her predicament and let out another shriek, using a word that Lola didn't even know she knew.

Lola bent her knees and then jumped into the air and grabbed a hold of Sassy. Luckily, they were in the shallow end, and as she reconnected with the base of the pool, Sassy was kept clear of the water.

"Thought you had sunk," Sassy said kissing Lola's face.

"No, sweetie, I'm still here." Lola kissed her back and climbed out of the water to see that a crowd had gathered around them, including Scott and Hart. Behind them, peeking from out of the changing rooms was Carmine.

"What was that all about?" Alice asked.

"I think she lost me," Lola said.

"Oh, come here, you silly goose." Alice took Sassy from Lola's arms and Tilly offered her a towel.

"Thanks."

"Not a goose, doggy." Sassy was shaking her head but she soon forgot as Alice took her back to the loungers for more cuddles.

"I brought a few biscuits for you, come on," Alice said.

All of Sassy's panic was gone and she was wiggling with delight so hard in Alice's arms that she almost wiggled free. Lola turned to see that Hart and Scott were still talking.

There was still a crack in the changing room doors and Lola imagined that Carmine was still trying to listen in on the conversation.

"Is there anything you can do for me?" Hart asked.

"I don't understand." Scott's brows were furrowed, his mouth open.

"Carmine is going to release to the press that I beat her. It would ruin me and I swear I didn't."

Scott looked down at his feet. "I don't want to get involved."

"Do you love her?" Hart asked. There was a touch of desperation in his voice.

Scott let out a harrumph. "Cool it man and don't be so stupid. I couldn't love a dried-up old prune like her. I'm just in it for the cash and the gifts, for what I can get. Once that goes I'm long gone and she can be all yours again."

Quicker than a Frenchie leaping into a swimming pool, Hart punched the younger man. "You disgust me."

Scott was back on his feet like a ninja and from out of nowhere he had the hunting knife in his hand. He slashed at Hart and the older man jumped back just in time to be missed. As he did, he went over on his ankle, and wheeling his arms he tipped back and back, landing in a heap on some empty chairs that scattered before him like he was a force of nature.

Scott moved with grace and speed and was over the fallen man. He raised the knife and swooped down with it, in what looked like a death blow.

Hart raised his hands and cowered away just as Lola reached out and grabbed Scott's wrist with the knife. She came face to face with Scott and he shrugged, dropped the knife, and turned to see Carmine standing behind him her face a mask of fury.

"Get out, you ungrateful pig. I will ruin you. I will set the press and the police on you. I never want to see your lying, sniveling face again."

Scott shrugged. "It was fun while it lasted, sayonara." He then turned to Hart. "Nice punch. For the right price, I will give you what you need. This crazy minx is the one who does the punching; I know and I have proof."

Carmine ran at Scott, beating her hands against his chest. He shrugged her off. "I guess you have proof now, too." With a chuckle, he walked away ducking into the men's changing rooms.

Carmine ran after him shrieking, but as she reached the door, a member of staff appeared and stood in her way. "Sorry, ma'am, this is men only."

Carmine let out a shriek of frustration and then ran from the room.

Hart was still lying in a pile of chairs, so Lola offered him her hand. "Are you all right?"

"Yes, thank you, thank you so much."

She helped him to his feet.

"I want to thank you for saving my life, you were very brave and incredibly quick. If there is anything I can do for you... I really appreciate your bravery."

Lola shook her head. "Actually, you were in no danger."

"I don't understand." Hart gave her a look that said she was clearly deranged.

"When I intercepted the blow, I should not have been able to stop it that quickly. He was just scaring you, he had already put the brakes on the movement. He would not have cut you."

"Ahh, I see. Though I'm not sure that makes me feel any better, I think I should report this."

"You had just assaulted the man." Lola raised an eyebrow and watched as her words sank in. The last thing she wanted was to have to give witness statements for this mess.

"Perhaps you're right. I'm leaving soon, anyway, so I should never see him again." With that, he limped away. It looked like he had hurt his ankle in the fall.

"It looks like I missed all the excitement."

Lola turned to see Linc grinning at her and she found herself returning the grin.

"Are you okay?" Linc asked.

"It was nothing, just two men butting heads, we women get used to it." She chuckled and was pleased when he joined her.

"Maybe I could treat you ladies to a coffee, in the conservatory?" he said over Lola's head to her group of friends who were all standing behind her. Lola noticed that Louisa and Sam were there also.

For a moment Lola was going to decline but Alice popped her head over her shoulder.

"As long as Carmine's not there, we're in," Alice said with a wink.

A big smile spread across Linc's face. "To new friendships. Ladies and gentleman." He bowed low and waved a hand in the direction of the stairs to the conservatory.

Her friends all surged ahead and Lola found herself walking with Linc. What had she let herself in for?

"Do you always attract this much trouble?" he asked.

Lola gave him a sharp look.

"I meant, this little one." He bent down and scooped Sassy into his arms.

"Like this man," Sassy said. "What sayonara mean?"

"Goodbye forever," Lola answered without thinking.

"Yes, he was a little dramatic," Linc said.

"You men have a penchant for it."

"Us men? Don't lump us all in with those two... idiots. I won't say the word that comes to mind, there are ladies present."

Lola grinned.

"Oh, I didn't mean you, I meant this one." He kissed Sassy on the forehead.

Lola chuckled again. Maybe this guy was going to be all right, but as she had that thought, a frisson of fear froze the blood in her veins.

CHOCOLATE

The conservatory was blissfully quiet. There was no sign of Carmine and Lola secretly hoped that she had left.

Louisa and Sam held hands in the corner and were whispering together. Lola gave them the occasional glance and wondered about Linc; he had taken all of their drinks orders and left them to find a waitress. Could something develop with him? Could she feel able to try a relationship again?

Sassy nuzzled against her leg and Lola looked down into her big expressive eyes. They were the most beautiful amber and were full of love. There was nothing in them that was hidden and Lola wished that people could be more like the dog. Why did people hide things?

* * *

"I think it's a great idea," Louisa whispered against Sam's ear. When they first met, he had seemed like such a nice boy, young and innocent and much too much of an innocent for her. It was not that she was that experienced, she was just a little world-weary, and although most people would have thought her snobby, for thinking such things, she was in fact, vulnerable. She had believed anyone as nice as Sam was too good for her. After all, she had almost been a kept woman at one stage, all be it, reluctantly.

Sam had helped her escape from that awful situation and that made him even more of a hero, at least in her eyes.

"What did you have in mind?" Sam asked and there was a twinkle in his deep brown eyes. She could look into those eyes forever.

"We will have to plan it well, Lola is no fool and we don't want her to see right through it."

"Do you think we should really do this, fake a murder?" Sam's eyes widened until they were surrounded by white.

"Why not, you know she will love it."

Sam nodded. "Ok, what sort of murder?"

"What are you two planning," Alice asked.

Sam and Louisa chuckled. "Just what we should do this afternoon," Sam said.

"The gym was great but we thought about exploring the grounds later," Louisa said.

"How about now?" Sam asked and they both stood.

"Hold your horses, Linc has just gone for drinks." Alice shook her head. "And they say it's the older generation that gets forgetful!" She winked at them and leaned forward to join in a conversation with Tilly and Tanya.

"Really, Jinny, if you don't get your act together you will be fired," Carmine's voice grated across Lola's nerves as she wafted into the conservatory.

"Oh, no," Lola mumbled. "Should we move? I can wait for Linc and tell him where we've gone."

Carmine was still walking and still moaning, sashaying straight through the conservatory to a door on the other side. "Maybe that is what's wrong, I have the wrong people around me, maybe I should make some changes?"

Jinny let out a moan. "No, please, I will do anything."

Carmine pushed through the door and let it go, nearly smacking Jinny in the face with it. She caught it at the last moment, dropping a number of papers in the process.

Lola felt a curl of anger growing inside her. What was wrong with the aging singer? Why did she treat people so badly?

Jinny scrabbled on the floor to pick them up and put a carrier bag with something heavy on a low glass table next to the door. Standing, she went through the door that looked like it opened into an office.

"Here we go," came Linc's deep voice.

Lola looked around to see him carrying a huge tray. On top of it were all their drinks in huge cups and plates of chocolates. As Linc bent, some of the coffee sloshed onto the tray. "Oh, no," he said.

"Let me." Tilly looked tiny next to him but she took the huge tray with ease and placed it on the low coffee table without spilling another drop. "Now, whose is whose?"

Lola had picked a caramel latte, Tilly a pot of tea, Alice and Louisa both had a cappuccino, Tanya had a flat white, Sam a glass of coke and Linc had an Americano. There was also a large plate of truffles.

"The chocolates are gin and champagne," Linc said with a conspiratol smile.

"Oh, let me." Alice grabbed one and then handed the plate around. "Take more than one," she said to Lola. "You need to put a bit of weight on those bones."

Lola laughed. "I've put loads on since I came to England."

"Save some for me," Sassy said.

"Sorry, pooch, chocolate's not good for dogs."

Sassy stuck out her bottom lip and looked most miserable.

"Don't you worry, little pup," Linc said. "The kitchen got me these doggy chocolates." He handed her one.

Sassy took it very gently and gave a little woof.

Lola heard, "He understands me, thanks Linc."

As the friends drank coffee, relaxed, and enjoyed the chocolates, people began to arrive to see Carmine. Scott was the first. Jinny showed him to a seat next to the table, she pointed out the carrier to him and then raised her nose as she walked back into the office.

Lola hadn't expected to see the man again. He had made his feelings clear and that had to have hurt Carmine. Why was he here now?

Lola noticed how his eyes traveled around the conservatory and settled on several groups of young women. There was something about the look on his face. It was predatory, not in a nasty, going to hurt them way, but in marks on the headboard way. He was also relaxed, whatever happened, happened. He wasn't stressing about getting back with Carmine or about the breakup. This had been entirely expected by him.

Jinny called, "You can come in."

Scott stood and as he approached the door, his face changed. It became more innocent. It was a little boy lost look, one that Carmine and Lola had no doubt lots of women found irresistible. They wanted to protect him.

Scott gave a jaunty rap on the door and walked in. The door didn't close and he didn't sit down. In just seconds, Jinny almost pushed him from the room. Scott took a seat on the nearest sofa and checked his watch. Though externally he looked confident, Lola could see his foot was now tapping on the floor. The man was now anxious about something.

"What is so interesting over there?" Linc asked.

"Sorry, it's nothing," Lola said and grabbed another chocolate off the plate that Alice was sharing around.

"She's looking for a mystery to solve," Tilly said. "Lola, here, is quite the detective."

Lola noticed a long-haired blonde shown into the room and the door closed behind her. Scott let out a sigh.

"Me too," Sassy barked.

"Really," Linc said handing Sassy a bit of the dog chocolate. "Tell me more."

"Well, I sniffies out the clues." Sassy pointed a paw at Lola. "She not use sniffies at all, how good your sniffies?"

Lola pulled her eyes away from Scott and stroked Sassy. There was no story there, he was just going to be dumped, and talking to Linc was becoming quite interesting.

"I think we'll take a stroll," Louisa said.

"Oh, why don't we all go?" Alice grabbed a couple of chocolates before she put the plate down.

Tilly kicked her ankle.

"Ouch," Alice said and gave her friend a sharp look.

"Let's finish the drinks and chocolates first," Tilly said.

"Oh, they can wait a few minutes." She waved at Louisa and Sam.

"Perhaps, they want a bit of time alone!"

"Oh, sorry." Alice raised her hands to her face covering her gaff before sitting down.

Louisa and Sam giggled and nodded their thanks to Tilly. "We will see you for lunch," Sam said and with his arm around Louisa, they walked out.

Across the room, the door to Carmine's meeting room slammed and the woman walked out in tears.

What was going on?

MISS BOSSY PANTS

Fred Stilby was the next one called into the office. The tension in his body was clear from across the room and the sound of raised voices could be clearly heard from inside.

"What is going on?" Lola asked.

"Carmine is known to be hard on the people who work with her," Alice said. "Rightly, in my opinion, she demands a high standard and the rumors are that she is clearing out her team and starting again. It must be awful to have such a light and then lose it."

"That's one way of putting it." Tilly rolled her eyes.

"How would you put it?" Lola asked.

"If I was them I would say good riddance to bad rubbish." Tilly folded her arms across her chest.

"Tilly, Carmine is not rubbish."

"Why don't we go to one of the rooms?" Tilly asked.

"What did you have in mind?" Lola was enjoying her conversation with Linc and wasn't sure she wanted to leave Sassy out of her sight.

I think I'll just read so I can keep my eye on Sassy," Tanya said. "You go and enjoy yourself."

"I love the salt room, or the herbal caldarium, ohh, or the rose-infused steam room. There's so much choice." Alice was perching on the edge of the sofa, her knees bouncing with excitement.

"I fancy the salt room," Tilly said.

Lola looked at Linc and he shrugged, "it beats sitting here and watching the stream of sad people go in and out to see Miss Bossy Pants over there."

"Okay, Sassy, can you look after Tanya?"

Linc laughed. "You talk to that dog as if she understands you and you her."

"She does." Lola smiled knowing he would think she was teasing. "Are you telling me you don't?"

Link chuckled. "Of course, I do, she wants another piece of chocolate."

"Wow," Sassy said, her eyes wide. "You can hear me."

Lola didn't have the heart to tell her trusty friend that Linc was teasing.

As they walked across the conservatory another victim walked into the office that Carmine was using. The man looked angry. He was short, around 5 foot 6, and plump which made him look even shorter. The cream suit he wore was a size too small and made him look a little like the Michelin tire man. Greasy black hair was combed over a bald spot and his pale skin made the red of anger on his cheeks even more prominent.

"That's Matt Wallens, Carmine's Digital Production Manager," Alice said. "Rumor is that he and she are having a lot of rows."

"I would say ex-Digital Production Manager," Lola said, looking at his body language.

* * *

The salt room was amazing. It was made out of pink Himalayan salt which lined the wall and was carved into benches. It was hot, but not unpleasant and in the corner was a salt basin piled high with salt nuggets that were producing steam.

Tilly and Alice sat next to each other and chatted about people in the village. Lola found herself tuning into the conversation as hers with Linc had dried up. It was funny to hear the two friends who never ran out of things to say but Lola was missing Sassy, she let out a breath of air.

"Is it too warm?" Linc asked.

"A little, should we...?" Lola was about to stand when Alice turned on her.

"Sit back down. You need to learn how to relax, you are staying still for ten minutes." Alice shook her head and then resumed her conversation with Tilly as if it had never been interrupted.

Lola shrugged and Linc chuckled.

"You have some good friends," he said.

"Thanks, how about you? It seems strange to see a man at a place like this all alone."

Linc sighed. "It was not my idea. I've been struggling a little recently and my best friend's wife thought a day here would do me good. I've been dreading it, I'm not used to sitting still."

"You and me both... but I've found it strangely enjoyable."

Linc winked. "I've enjoyed my day, so far, but I don't think it's strange. I've been in good company."

Lola blushed and was pleased that the muted light and rose glow in the room should hide it from him.

"I do mean Sassy, of course, and the entertainment provided by Carmine and her phone."

Lola laughed out loud and it felt good. "Tell me about yourself."

A glazed look crossed his face and he swallowed. "You might not like it."

"It's okay," she said. "I guessed you are military, a veteran."

"Yeah, not long back and it's still difficult to talk about. Excuse me, I could do with some air." With that, he got up and left the room.

Lola was stunned, it was not what she expected from the confident man but she understood.

"Where did he go?" Alice asked.

"Just for some air, we'll meet up later." Lola said the words, but she wasn't sure if that would be the case. Maybe it was for the best; she liked Linc, but people who got close to her always got hurt.

NOT QUITE LUNCH

As Lola, Alice and Tilly made their way back to the conservatory they saw Tanya stretched out on the sofa reading with Sassy curled up on her lap. It seemed that Lola didn't need to worry about her little pal.

"Would anyone like some cucumber water?" Alice asked.

"Sure," Lola said and the others all nodded.

"I'll get it." Alice was off like a flash to the dispenser in the corner of the room. There were lots of the dispensers dotted throughout the spa. Lola imagined it was because of the heat. Although it was very pleasant, the last thing people needed was to get dehydrated.

Sassy crawled off Tanya's knee and without standing up crawled onto Lola's and promptly fell back to sleep. Lola could hear some of her thoughts, she was hunting a blackbird that came into the garden, "Slowly, slowly, keep low. Don't let birdy see you. Slowly, just one more step. Run!" Her little legs were twitching as if she was racing across the lawn after the feathered intruder.

Lola stroked her and she seemed to relax but didn't wake.

Lola had positioned herself so that she was looking over at the door to the room Carmine was using. Scott was still sitting outside, his eyes roving the room and spending a good amount of time on a group of girls across from him. They were enjoying his surveillance and giggled from time to time.

The door opened and Jinny waved Scott inside.

The sound of raised voices, well, one raised voice. Carmine's could be heard through the open door. "Out, get out, you ungrateful weasel."

Scott came out of the room, and though his jaw was tense, he walked, well, strutted, straight across to the party of young ladies, where he was invited to join them.

Such loyalty, Lola thought but there was more shouting going on in the room. The door burst open and Jinny ran out with tears streaming down her face as she fled across the conservatory.

"Oh, look! It's only an hour until lunchtime," Alice said. "Why don't we order and then spend a bit of time by the pool before we come back up."

Lola checked her watch and sure enough, it was. As they made their way along the corridors she found herself looking for Linc and was disappointed when she didn't see him. Was it suspicious? Part of her understood him not wanting to talk about his experiences in the military. There were plenty of her own she didn't want to relive with every Tom, Dick, or Harry she met in a spa, but the way he behaved seemed off. It was as if he had something to be ashamed of and he was worried that she might find it out. No, that was silly, she was reading too much into it. Maybe, like her, he didn't want to get too close.

As they arrived at the restaurant the tables that had been set up for breakfast were gone and a waiter gave them menus. "The other two members of your party have already chosen," he said as he led them through to a small room with just three tables and seated them next to a smiling Sam and Louisa. The two of them looked as if they had a secret. It was bursting out of them as they tried to keep a straight face.

"Once you have chosen your meals, come back at the appointed time to these tables."

"What have you two been up to?" Alice asked as she sat next to Sam and opposite Louisa.

"We've been exploring the grounds. They are quite extensive and very interesting," Louisa said hiding a giggle behind her hands.

"Then we had a go at archery with a man called Simon," Sam said. "It was really cool, I think I might even take it up. I bet you lot have just been sitting around doing nothing." He smirked but it was not unfriendly.

"Us oldies, you mean." Tilly raised an eyebrow and watched as his face turned red and he began to stutter.

"I... I... I didn't mean that."

Tilly laughed. "I know, I was just teasing."

The menu was superb and Lola chose minted lamb shanks, with red wine, mustard, and honey sauce along with mashed kumara and petit pois. They all chose what they were having and then made their way downstairs to the loungers by the pool.

"I'm going to Yoga," Tanya said. "Toodles."

Lola was still scanning for Linc but he was nowhere to be seen. Had he left? If so, she had no contact details for him. Maybe that was for the best.

"You looking for chocolate man," Sassy said. "Can't sniffies him."

"Who?" she said and Tilly raised an eyebrow.

Lola shrugged her shoulders, maybe she should tell her friends that she could hear Sassy talking? No, she had only ever told one person and she was not ready for the looks she would get.

"Linc, chocolate man, he nice," Sassy said. "He not in here."

Lola wanted to deny it but she knew there was no point. Sassy could somehow read her emotions off her scent and she would know. She wasn't sure how she felt about looking for him but she couldn't deny she had been.

Lola relaxed back and closed her eyes and before she knew it she had nodded off.

The sound of Jinny shouting cut through the quiet and relaxing day. "Where is she, where is Carmine?" Jinny rushed into the pool area. "Have you seen, Carmine?" she shrieked at a couple.

They shook their heads and Jinny made her way to the next group when a male member of staff came over to her. He was talking calmly and escorted a weeping Jinny from the pool.

"Oh, I am so sorry," Alice said. "I love Carmine but I hate that she has spoiled things for you all."

"She hasn't," Tilly said.

"No, ignore all this, we're having a great time," Lola said.

"Forget her," Tanya added as she walked back after her yoga class.

Their eyes turned to Sam and Louisa who were whispering again. The young couple stopped and looked guilty. "Jinny's maybe screaming because someone murdered Carmine," Sam said with a wink.

"Don't even think it." Alice had turned as white as a sheet.

Lola looked at Sam, studying him. He really was up to something, but what?

HOT TUB BLUES

The friends relaxed at the side of the pool. Tilly and Alice were reading. Sam and Louisa had gone for another walk and Tanya had her eyes closed.

Lola let out a groan as she noticed the angry ginger-headed man who had been with Carmine that morning walking through the pool area. The tension in his body language was easy to read. His fists were clenched, and the expensive suit that set him apart from everyone else was looking a little disheveled. There was a touch of red on his pinched cheeks and he was walking fast. Behind him came Hart and three attractive blonde women. They all had long hair and despite the luxurious robes, looked fit and slim, athletic even. One of them had been crying, Lola thought, as she wiped at her eyes.

Hart looked despondent. They walked through the pool area and out the other side and were gone from her view.

"No angry bird," Sassy said. "Just angry people."

"It seems to have been a day for tempers," Lola said and stroked Sassy. Part of her wanted to get up and go talk to the people but why? There was no mystery, just a mind that didn't want to relax. In the end, she closed her eyes and tried to sleep.

Lola drifted off to sleep quicker than she expected. The heat took her back to the desert and she began to twitch as images of war flashed across her mind.

A touch of dampness on her cheek brought her back to the present with a jump. Lola opened her eyes to see Sassy sitting over her.

"No bad dream," Sassy said and kissed her again.

"Where is she?" Jinny shrieked as she rushed into the pool area. "Where is Carmine?"

Lola sat up, it looked like their relaxation time was over.

"Miss, please calm down." A tall distinguished member of staff walked over to Jinny. "Miss Rivers is out at the stones with a group of her friends."

"No, they have all come back. Something has happened to her, I can't find her."

"Let me help you look," the man said as he steered the lost-looking Jinny out of the pool area. There was something defeated about her and Lola hoped that she would just go and leave the singer behind. There was something unhealthy in the way she doted on the older woman.

"How long is it until lunch?" Louisa asked.

"We can go up between 1 and 2. It's 12.40 so we have a bit of time, I thought we'd go closer to 2 after all the chocolates." Tilly said without raising her eyes from her book.

"Let's all go in the hot tubs in case Jinny makes another hysterical appearance," Tanya said. "It would be nice to have a quick soak, and then come back in here to relax before lunch."

Nods of agreement went around the group but Lola was itching to go see what Jinny was upset about. It had looked like she had been fired earlier, and now it was as if she was worried for Carmine. That didn't make sense to her. Maybe, she could help the woman leave Carmine behind? Why was it that her brain was constantly looking for a mystery?

"No, you don't," Tanya said, and linking her arm with Lola's, she dragged her out onto the patio.

Lola chuckled as she was pulled along, it seemed her friends knew her too well.

There was a lovely area in full sunshine surrounded by gloriously scented deep red roses. Union Jack bunting was draped around the building and pinned along a fence that kept the hot tubs sheltered.

"Oh, they still have the jubilee bunting up." Alice spun around in a circle her arms wide, her orange robe catching the wind and fluttering around her like a fluorescent ballgown. "Doesn't it look wonderful?"

"It does, I did enjoy the jubilee," Lola said. "It was just so... regal." It had been out of this world for her. The pomp, the ceremony, the Queen and royal family all so... she didn't have the words to describe it. Magnificent, regal, royal... all came to mind, but she had loved every minute of it as well as the parties. The village had put on a big jubilee party along with a cake competition. Jealousy had almost spoiled the day but Sassy came to the rescue, along with her friend, the rescue boxer, Tyson.

"It was wonderful," Tilly said. "I've enjoyed them all, but the 25th and this one were my favorite."

"Oh, yes, I heard that the street parties in 1977 were just amazing," Alice said. "I wish I had been there."

Lola had her robe and a towel for Sassy to lie on. "Where do you want to be?" she asked.

Sassy was glancing at the roses and out to the garden. "I go chase birdies." Her eyes were wide, her mouth open and her tongue hanging out in anticipation.

"Not just yet, but we will go for a walk, later." Lola stroked Sassy behind the ears and placed the robe in an area close to the hot tub but in direct sunlight. Sassy liked to sunbathe.

Sassy took one last glance at the garden before curling up on the robe with a bit of a harumph. She was, however, soon snoring.

The hot tub was divine. It smelled of Jasmine and as they stepped into the toasty water, it was like being cocooned in loving warmth.

"How are you coping with doing nothing?" Tilly asked as she sat down next to Lola.

"The day has gone surprisingly quickly." Lola noticed Linc walking from the area of the Zen garden and past the rose bushes. His head was down and he didn't see them. Where had he been, what had he been up to? He didn't go toward the building but back out to the garden. There was something defensive about his posture. Part of her wanted to go after him, to apologize, to see if she could talk to him some more, but it was not the time. At least, he hadn't left. Maybe they would meet later.

They spent a good 10 minutes, relaxing, chatting, and giggling in the hot tub. Alice made every experience one of delight. The bubbles caused her swimsuit to fill up with air and she floated around laughing with sheer joy. Once the jets stopped they were too hot and climbed out and into the soft fluffy towels.

"Ohh, time for 40 minutes relaxing before lunch," Alice said and headed back to the loungers.

At the same time, Louisa and Sam were walking together holding hands and giggling and Lola found it so cute.

"Isn't this just wonderful?" Alice said as they all lay on the sun loungers next to the pool drinking more of the cucumber water.

Lola nodded. The place was amazing, like a tropical jungle inside with beautiful foliage and such warmth that you just wanted to relax and indulge.

"Should we go for lunch?" Alice asked. "I'm starting to get peckish."

"Need wee wees," Sassy said as Lola stretched out her legs and adjusted her robe.

Tilly looked up from her book. It was Tilly Trotter Alone by Catherine Cookson. They had all laughed when she pulled it out of her bag. Tilly was famous for telling people that she was not the famous Tilly Trotter but who knows if Catherine Cookson named her character after her. "I think we can go along in about 15 minutes."

"I'll just take Sassy out for a quick walk," Lola said. The Frenchie needed a walk and she wanted to cool down, It was lovely to sit here but she felt that a touch of fresh air would do her good.

"Should we all go?" Tanya asked.

Lola had thought she was asleep as her eyes had been closed and she was lying back.

"I don't mind the company."

"Then it's agreed."

They walked outside, past the hot tubs, and through the rose garden.

"Bally," Sassy said jumping up and down in front of Sam.

"How does she know?" he asked.

"He understands me," Sassy said her eyes wide open.

"I think she can smell it." Lola didn't have the heart to tell Sassy that Sam had just guessed. The little dog was always hoping that she would have more people to talk to. Lola chuckled, if anyone could hear her thoughts they would think her crazy. Could she really hear Sassy talking or was it just in her mind?

Thinking about it, she decided it didn't matter, what harm was it doing?

Sam pulled the tennis ball from the pocket of his gown and threw it as they walked. Sassy raced after it bringing it back and dropping it at his feet.

"Not too much, you can have some more later," Lola said. It was a hot day and she didn't want Sassy to get too warm.

Sassy jumped up and down in front of Sam but he shook his head and put the ball back in his pocket.

Lola was still surprised at how nice the weather was in England. Sure, it did rain and sometimes hard and for days. Sometimes the rain was cold and the wind strong but mostly it was all very pleasant. Today was no exception. The sun beat down from above them. There was a slight breeze that cooled the skin and brought with it the scent of roses.

"I wanted to tell you about the trees in the right-hand corner of the gardens. I think you will be fascinated," Alice said falling in step with Lola.

They were walking across a large grass area, a blackbird was looking for worms just in front of them.

"Yeeeeahhhhh," Sassy let out a shriek and raced after the bird.

The blackbird seemed to look and waited until the last moment before lazily taking to the air and calling out a warning. Sassy jumped up, her teeth snapping on nothing as the bird flew away.

"So close," Sassy said as she ran back.

"There you go." Alice was pointing across the beautifully mown grass, so green and vibrant, to a group of three trees in the distance.

Lola had seen them before, briefly, and was confused, as they looked like Redwoods. They were very tall, but not as thick as those she had seen back home, surely, they couldn't be. "Are they...?"

"Yes." Alice was nodding. "Aren't they magnificent?"

They were walking closer and Lola was stunned. Though the trees were not as large as the ones back in the US, they were indeed impressive. Her mouth dropped open.

"You'll catch flies," Sassy said and then ran off after another bird.

"Are they Redwoods?" Lola managed to ask.

"Well," there was a twinkle in Alice's eye. "They are actually Wellingtonia Gigantean, named by Prof John Lindley of the Horticultural Society of London to commemorate the Duke of Wellington after his death."

Lola felt her mouth open even more just as Sassy ran back and pawed at her leg. Ignoring her, Lola followed

Alice towards the trees. Sassy pawed at her leg again. "Bally later," Lola said. This seemed to work and Sassy ran to Sam.

"Not just yet, 10 minutes," he said.

Louisa laughed. "Now, you are talking to that dog like she understands you."

"I'm sure she does." Sam chuckled. "Look at her, how can you say she doesn't understand me?"

"You're all mad," Louisa said and chuckled.

"Tell me about the trees?" Lola encouraged Alice as she could see her friend was desperate to share her knowledge of their history.

"Smellie something," Sassy said. "Something bad."

Lola laughed, the Frenchie was always smelling something bad or good depending on her mood that day. She was sure it was nothing, probably just a dead bird or some cow poop.

CONTROVERSIAL TREES

"So they are not Redwoods?" Lola asked.

Alice's eyes sparkled and she smiled. "Well, actually, they are now called *Sequoiadendron giganteum* to reflect the tree's botanical link to another giant tree: the coastal or California redwood, *Sequoia sempervirens*.

"The dispute about this raged for years. But as I know it, this is their history. They were discovered in 1852 when plant hunter William Lobb heard about some vast trees growing in the foothills of California's Sierra Nevada range."

They walked a little closer. Sassy seemed to have forgotten the scent and was circling Sam for her ball. He was too busy with Louisa and once more they were whispering and giggling. Lola kept one ear on Alice but she was sure these two were up to some trickery or other.

"There was a growing market among gentlemen enthusiasts in England for huge and new plants and trees. The more spectacular, the better. To this effect, Lobb collected seeds and specimens and returned home with them. They sold out almost instantly on his return. Saplings were planted all over the country including these here. You can still buy seeds, but I'm told that getting them through the first 5 years is very difficult. If they make it to 5 they are hardy and suited to the climate."

Lola didn't think there was anything sinister in Sam or Louisa's behavior but she was curious, or maybe she was just jealous of their closeness.

"Lobb told prospective purchasers how he had found these towering trees that reached up to the heavens. He had drawings of one felled tree that measured 300 feet with a diameter of more than 29 feet near its base. It was thought to be 3,000-years-old. This tree was displayed in San Francisco. A piano was placed inside its hollowed and carpeted trunk, and an audience of 40 could be seated inside in comfort."

"Throw bally," Sassy said jumping up in front of Sam.

"However, in the US and the UK, the race was on to give this newly discovered giant a name. Dr. Albert Kellogg wanted to name it the Washingtonia in honor of the nation's first president." Alice chuckled and her eyes sparkled once more, she was enjoying this. "In England, Professor John Lindley of the Horticultural Society of London opted for the decidedly un-American "Wellingtonia Gigantean" to commemorate the recently deceased Duke of Wellington. This was greeted with much indignation in America."

"I bet it was." Lola chuckled, it was good to see Alice so enthused and she wondered how she managed to know everything about wherever they visited.

"Bally!" Sassy barked.

"Can she have it yet?" Sam asked.

"Sure. I guess we should start to walk back anyway."

They turned along the hedgerow that separated the garden from the roadway. Tanya and Tilly were walking ahead, Alice and Lola together and Sam and Louisa to one side. Sam pulled out the tennis ball and Sassy jumped in the air. Her short stubby legs carried her surprisingly high but there was no way she could get the ball.

Sam teased her with it and then threw it as far as he could.

Sassy raced after the ball, almost a lilac blur across the grass. She picked it up without slowing and then slammed on the brakes, turned, and ran back.

After the third throw, Sassy dropped the ball and raised her nose into the air. "Oh, oh," she said and set off in the direction of the hedgerow that surrounded the garden.

"What is it?" Sam asked and everyone turned to look at Lola.

She didn't know what it was but she knew Sassy had smelt something and so she followed the little dog.

When they got there, Sassy was working her way into the hedge.

"Stop her, the road's the other side of that hedge," Tilly called.

"Sassy!" Lola felt a stab of fear in her heart as adrenaline raced along her arms raising the hair there. She could hear the traffic and if what Sassy smelt was on the other side of the road... it didn't bear thinking about.

Lola dropped to her knees and peered into the hedge. Sassy was just in front of her, could she reach her and pull her back? "Come on out, it's dangerous."

The hedge was hawthorn and covered in nasty spikes. Lola reached in but she couldn't get ahold of Sassy. "Come on, out now." Panic was rising inside of her.

"Just a bit further," Sassy said.

Lola watched the little tail disappear down a slight slope and pushed further into the hedge. A thorn caught her arm through the robe and drew blood but still, she reached further. "Sassy, come back."

"Got it!" Sassy wiggled backward out of the hedge.

Lola backed out before letting go of a big breath of air, the danger was over and she could relax.

Sassy turned to face them, a vicious-looking blood-covered knife clenched between her little teeth.

THE DISCOVERY

Lola felt her pulse kick up a notch but Alice was laughing and shaking a finger at Sam and Louisa.

"Has anyone got a plastic bag on them?" Lola asked. She bent down and stroked Sassy. "Well done, girl."

Sassy was still holding the knife and looked so proud of her accomplishment.

"It's just these two," Alice said pointing at Sam and Louisa. "I heard them plotting this and it might be fun, but I'm hungry."

"I have a bag with some sun lotion in it." Tanya produced the bag from her pocket.

It wasn't quite big enough, but Lola turned it inside out and took the knife off Sassy. It was expensive and distinctive. The blade was made of Damascus steel. Easily recognizable by the wavy pattern in the metal. It was expensive, very expensive. Aside from its sleek look and beautiful aesthetics, Damascus steel was highly valued for its strength and flexibility while maintaining a razor-sharp edge. Weapons forged from Damascus steel were far superior to those formed from just iron.

The handle was bone with two gold mosaic pins. Whoever had lost this must be looking for it... unless it was a fake.

"It wasn't us, I swear," Sam said but he chuckled and looked at Louisa. She shook her head.

"Don't lie, I heard you talking about faking a murder for Lola, didn't I?" Alice asked them, her face was stern, and her gaze pinned Sam to the spot.

San nodded. "Well... well, yes, but..."

"There we have it, there's no mystery here. Let's go eat."

Alice, Tilly, and Tanya had already started walking back. Lola bent down to Sassy. "Is this blood?"

"Yes, blood of angry bird."

Lola chuckled, so it was bird blood, perhaps a hunter had lost his knife. That seemed strange as the vicious-looking knife looked new and a little familiar. It was much too expensive to have been discarded. However, Alice was probably right, Sam & Louisa had planted this just to get her wondering. “Very funny, you two,” Lola said as she tucked the bagged knife into her gown and began the walk back.

“I swear, this wasn’t us. We had planned a murder but we used an old scarecrow and got the gardener to help. We were going to take you over there this afternoon.”

Lola chuckled. “It doesn’t matter, the blood is bird blood so there’s no mystery here.”

“We need to look for angry bird,” Sassy said. “Could be hurt.”

Lola picked her up. “We can look later, it’s time for lunch.”

Sassy glanced back at the hedge. “Can’t sniffy angry bird, okay, do I get sausage?”

Lola snuggled into Sassy’s neck. “How about a bit of lamb?”

* * *

The meals were wonderfully cooked and quickly served along with tea and coffee. Conversation flowed easily but Lola noticed that Louisa and Sam were looking worried. Were they annoyed that their plot had so easily been discovered? She was sure of it, and yet, something felt wrong. Maybe, her analytical mind had been looking for a mystery and felt cheated. After all, her pulse had raced when she saw Sassy with the knife, she did enjoy solving a good mystery.

Color touched her cheeks and she shook her head, what was it with her? Wanting there to be a murder just so she could have a little excitement was just wrong.

During the meal, Sassy made her way around the table begging for bits of food from all of them. Luckily, the other tables in the room were empty and the little Frenchie worked her magic and managed to get something off every plate. Eventually, she came back to sit in front of Lola. Dropping her butt to the floor, she stuck out her back legs and promptly belched.

Lola laughed, and Sassy looked a little put out. "It's a sign of appreciation."

Lola chuckled. "Who told you that?" she whispered while bending down.

"Tony."

That made sense, Tony Munch was a lovely man with a wonderful rescue boxer dog called Tyson. It was the sort of thing she could imagine him saying and Sassy had picked it up. The little dog had a habit of picking up on the quirk of people's vocabulary.

"Who's for dessert?" Alice asked.

Sassy let out a big whine of "Me, me, me." She spun in a circle and then stopped, dropping to the floor and covering her eyes with her paws. "They're not going to eat me are they?"

Lola chuckled.

Lola opted for a cheese plate so she could share a little bit with Sassy and she was feeling quite full after the lamb. Her mind kept going back to the knife and why it was in the hedge.

Lola kept thinking about the knife. She had put it in her locker and everyone else had forgotten about it but it was nagging at her brain. Why was it there? Who did it belong to? Why did it have bird blood on it?

The sound of tears and wailing cut through the quiet room and all eyes were drawn to the corridor. Jinny was being consoled by a member of staff. The man looked desperate to get her out of the corridor.

"Where is she?" Jinny sobbed.

"I'm sure she just left, why don't you go back to my office and I will look around for you again."

"But she wouldn't leave me, I'm her driver." Jinny fumbled in her pockets eventually pulling out a large bunch of keys, including the keyless key of a Mercedes. "I have the keys, she has to be here and I'm so worried."

"I know." The man consoled Jinny keeping perfectly calm unlike some of the people at their table. "I will look for her, I promise, just come this way." The man cast them an apologetic glance.

Sam was chuckling and shaking his head. "The angry bird sacks her, and now she's worried that she can't find her."

"What did you say?" Lola had a bad feeling about this.

THE MISSING ANGRY BIRD

"Carmine, or whatever her name is," Sam said. "We nicknamed her Angry Bird because, well, because she always seemed angry."

"Blood was from the angry bird," Sassy said, her words muffled as she was licking some cream cheese off her teeth. "Told you!"

"Did Sassy hear you call her that?" Lola asked and then stopped as the whole of the table was looking at her as if she was a sandwich short of a picnic. "Well, you see, she... Sassy indicated that it was bird blood on the knife... but that could have been Carmine's if she heard you."

Sam laughed so hard that he almost spat out a profiterole. Apologizing profusely he clutched his belly until he could speak. "I don't think a dog could quite get the gist of a nickname and use that to indicate bird blood instead of human blood."

"Can too!" Sassy was pouting, her bottom lip out, her eyes sad.

"I can't believe a dog could tell the difference," Louisa said. "You are so funny with the way you talk to her but you don't believe it... do you?"

Lola flushed; was her secret finally out? Should she just admit it? No, it was not the time and no one would believe her. If it got back to Wayne then she might lose some of her police contacts. It was best to just rise over this. "They can discern what blood it is. Their noses and the area of the brain that processes scent is much larger than in humans."

"Oh, don't be silly. No way could a dog... with that small a nose... work out what blood that was if it wasn't tomato sauce." Sam was looking a little incredulous.

"Can too, not Tommy sauce, would have lickied that."

This was back on safer ground and Lola hoped that a few explanations would move the conversation away from her sanity. "Dogs can discern if it is human blood or animal from just a tiny sample or even from a piece of bone. Their sense of smell is amazing, they can detect a teaspoon of sugar in a million gallons of water. They can detect a body below 30 meters of water or buried 15 feet underground." Lola noticed that her friends were looking at her with wide-eyed amazement. "Sorry, I get carried away."

"But you thought it was bird blood on the knife," Sam said and scratched his head. "How did you know?"

Lola could hardly tell them that Sassy had told her it was angry bird blood. Looking down she could see Sassy pointing with her front left paw. "Pointing," she said.

"She was taught to indicate birds by pointing, i.e., holding up a front paw," Lola said.

"Well then, there you have it, the knife had bird blood on it," Tilly said. "I fancy going to the yoga relaxation session, anyone coming?"

"Oh goody." Alice clapped her hands. "But don't start snoring this time."

"I didn't."

"Oh, you did."

"We're going to have a swim," Louisa said.

"I'm going for a facial," Tanya added.

"Well, in that case, we might have a walk and explore more of the grounds. I'm sure Sassy will enjoy the sunshine." Lola hoped she had got away with it but she needed to be more careful. The problem was she heard Sassy as clear as any of them and it was just natural to answer her.

"See if you can find that nice man and tell him we owe him a coffee later." Alice winked.

Lola nodded and looked away quickly as she could feel her cheeks glowing.

* * *

Lola and Sassy looked in all the rooms where diners were seated and then wandered up to the conservatory. Scott had gone and so had the women he was with. The door to the room Carmine had used was closed so Lola tried it and saw that it was just a small office. No one was there. She checked the rooftop terrace but Carmine was not there either. No doubt, Jinny had already checked all of these places but perhaps Carmine was actively avoiding her, she would not do the same to Lola.

Lola ambled down to the gym and checked the relaxation room but did not see what she was looking for. Next, they went to the swimming pool and treatment rooms. She told herself she was looking for Carmine, but in truth, she was hoping to catch a glimpse of Linc, but it didn't matter, neither of them was to be found. Lola felt a little disappointed but something else was growing inside of her. So far she hadn't asked Sassy if the blood on the knife was Carmine's, but she knew she had to. No one was around so she squatted down.

"This is important."

Sassy sat and looked up at her, her amber eyes wide and giving her their full attention. They always filled Lola with love, and this time was no different. She could face anything with her little friend at her side.

"Sassy, the blood on the knife, was it the angry lady's blood?"

"Yes, angry bird."

Oh, dear, that did change things. "Let's go see if we can find her."

"Sniffies on high alert, I do good." Sassy raced to the door and out past the hot tubs. Lola was having to jog to keep up with her. Sassy raced across the wide-open area of grass back to where she had found the knife.

Lola looked all around and then she noticed someone standing amongst the redwood trees. Were they hiding? It was Linc, when he saw her watching he waved and stepped out of the shadow.

Sassy was taking in great gulps of air and sniffing really loudly. "Can't find more," she said and wandered away along the hedge.

"Don't go under the hedge, come to me first," Lola said as Linc drew near.

"I'm sorry I ran off like that," he said. "It's just... well..."

"There's no need to explain, I've been there." She touched his arm and smiled. The man looked to have aged 5 years and there were deep bags under his eyes.

"I want to tell you but I don't want to sound like... a wimp... or... well... I guess I wanted to impress you and this wouldn't."

Lola chuckled. "Don't worry, but right now, I have to follow Sassy."

"Lead on, mind if I join you?"

"Not at all." Lola wondered how she could explain that her talking dog had found a hunting knife with blood on it and that she was using a French Bulldog, the dog with probably the smallest nose in the canine kingdom to see if she could track down a body."

"You seem distracted," Linc said.

"This is going to sound strange but Sassy found a blood-covered knife and Carmine is missing."

"A posh bone-handled hunting knife with a Damascus steel blade, by any chance?"

Lola didn't quite know what to say to that and her mouth must have dropped open. Was the knife Linc's, was that why he disappeared? The man certainly had the skills to dispatch Carmine. Lola felt her instincts kick in, she had to be careful and yet, her gut told her to trust him.

Linc chuckled. "I saw the knife earlier, it was a gift from Carmine to her boyfriend, the one she heard saying she was... what was it... oh, yes, an old prune. The one she gave the push earlier."

"Well, that is interesting," Lola said.

"Oh, oh, I sniffies angry bird blood." Sassy was already racing along sniffing the air.

For just a moment, Lola wondered if she would ever get the chance to relax, then she shrugged at Linc and raced after Sassy.

ANGRY BIRD DOWN

They raced along the hedge and to the far corner of the garden. There were some large rhododendron bushes, not currently in flower, screening off the corner, and in front of them was a small stone circle.

Lola didn't think the stone circle was genuine, it was more than likely, a folly, built by the hall as a feature. Twelve rough-hewn stones of around 2 feet high were placed around a center stone that was about 5 feet high.

Sassy went around the circle sniffing at each stone and then to the rhododendron bushes. Lola followed her, but there was nothing there.

Sassy disappeared beneath one of the bushes and then let out what would sound to Linc like a bark. To Lola, it said, "Angry bird down."

"Oh, dear," Lola said and dropped down onto her knees.

"What are you doing?"

Lola looked back to see a strange expression on Linc's face. It was part fear and part curiosity. Why would this affect him like that? He must have seen many things, for she had spoken to him earlier, and he had served in the British Army.

"Sassy has found something, I think it could be Carmine."

Linc stepped back. "We should go and leave this, let someone else deal with it." The minute he said the words his face changed, shame flashed across his handsome features and then he shook his head. "I'm sorry, what I meant was if something is there you shouldn't contaminate the scene."

"I understand, but I can hardly tell the police that my French Bulldog thinks there is a body in the bushes, now can I?" She raised her eyebrows but before he could say anything else, she crawled under the greenery.

"Hey," Sassy said, her tongue hanging out. "Not been here long, and deaded nearby... that way." Sassy pointed her nose out the other side of the bush which was much easier to get to. Lola knew that her hair would be raked all over and she was covered in soil and leaves.

"Good girl."

Sassy rolled over and let Lola stroke her belly. The little dog was stressed, she couldn't ignore the scent of blood, it would lead her to the scene every time but it always upset her and she needed the contact for comfort.

There was an overriding strong scent, that at first, Lola couldn't recognize, then she realized it was patchouli, used in some countries to disguise the scent of death.

Lola continued to stroke Sassy while peering deeper into the bush. Sure enough, Carmine was lying there. She looked quite serene, her fur-embellished robe was arranged perfectly around her. The scent was even stronger now and Lola wondered how Sassy had smelt anything over it.

In some ways, Carmine looked a little bit like sleeping beauty. There was no discernable injury though her face was pale.

"Come on," Lola said and Sassy led the way out of the bushes.

Lola stood up to see Linc's eyes widen. She ran a hand over her hair, though it was long, black, and straight it had a mind of its own and she imagined that she looked a little like the wild woman of Borneo or a British TV character called Wurzel Gummage,

Linc leaned forward and wiped a smudge off her cheek. "I thought you were gone for a moment." He chuckled.

Lola wasn't sure how to take his behavior, one moment he was confident, the next nervous, did he have something to hide?

"It was quite overgrown in there but we have to call the police."

"Oh!" His face dropped and he turned a little green for a moment.

"Are you okay?" she asked and noticed that Sassy was leaning against his leg. This was her sign that the person was upset and needed her comfort.

"I guess... well, I had... I hoped I'd left all this behind." His hand waved at the bush.

Lola nodded. “I don’t have my phone, I left it in my locker.”

“I do,” he said and pulled a phone out of his robe’s pocket. From then on his training showed. “Is it Carmine?”

“Yes.”

“Was it murder?”

Lola thought back to the scene. The body had looked so peaceful. There was no blood but the robe was over her. Could there be blood beneath it? She shook her head, of course, it was murder, she hardly crawled under there and passed away. “I can’t say for sure, but the knife, her being under the bushes...”

“Yeah, but was there a wound?”

“I couldn’t see.”

“Yes,” Sassy said and pawed Lola’s leg. “Lots of blood same as on knife.”

“I think there was blood but it was tight under there and would be easier to get to from the other side.” Lola began to walk around but Linc grabbed her shoulder.

"Let's leave it to the police," he said. He dialed 999. "Police," he said when they asked him which service. There was an edge to his voice but he remained calm. "My name is Martin Hall, I'm with Lola Ramsay at The Clinton Day Spa, we have found a body that we think is Carmine Rivers and it looks to be foul play."

Lola listened as Lincoln gave a few more details and was told to wait for them. He suggested that the police come in quietly and unmarked if possible and that they met them in the car park.

Lola felt more reassured, it looked as if he knew a little about procedure and was determined not to warn any potential suspects. Now, she had to find out a way to get on the case. The murder had to be solved.

"Why don't you meet the police and I'll protect the scene?" Lola said.

Linc smiled. "You wouldn't be going to look around for clues, would you?"

"No, of course not. I'll just stand out of sight and watch for any suspicious behavior."

"I believe you," he said with a smile before he turned and walked away.

Lola knew she didn't have long but she would gather what evidence she could. Who could have done this? The singer had upset a lot of people today, but surely, not enough to murder her. Could it even be Linc? After all, he was found in the garden near where the knife was discovered and he was missing at the time of the murder. There was no doubt that he had the skill. Lola groaned, she didn't want to think this way but she had to keep an open mind.

THE SCARE IN THE BUSHES

Lola wandered around the rhododendron bushes until she found the other side. All the time she was careful where she stood and checked for any evidence that might be there.

There was nothing that she could see, just a few broken branches where Carmine had been moved to her resting place. Lola squatted down to see if she could discern anything but without moving the clothing she couldn't and that might disturb evidence so she decided to do nothing.

"Can you smell anything?" Lola asked. She doubted that Sassy would be able to tell her much as the air was filled with the scent of patchouli. As she thought about that it pulled her mind back to Linc. He had been in

Afghanistan and would know what the oil was used for over there. Was it evidence against him?

For a moment she hated her mind. It was always weighing up the clues and trying to work out where they led. At the moment, she didn't know Linc well enough to be able to discount him as a suspect. She wanted to, but she couldn't and that was an entirely unpleasant thought.

"Lots of sniffies," Sassy said. "Angry bird, but lots of people from inside."

"Does one stand out?"

"Nice man," Sassy said. "His is strongest."

Lola felt her stomach tumble, but it didn't mean that Linc was involved. Of course, his scent would be the strongest, he had only just left here.

Looking over at the building, she took a moment to admire it. The tall chimneys, the central turret, the beautiful stone. It was a perfect picture of English country life, well, the life of the gentry. To the side, she saw Linc and two men walking across the grass. It was time to stand back and just guard the scene.

"Good day, I'm Detective Sergeant Eades and this is Constable Wilson. Now, what do we have here?" The man to the right of Linc was 5 feet 9 inches and looked tired and a little bored. His greying hair was cut short and combed back. A slightly red face and neck said he had indulged in a little too much sun recently. He was wearing a cheap but neat brown suit that was work-like and practical. It told her that the man wasn't looking to impress and right now he thought that this was a hoax.

On the other side of Linc was a young constable with a fresh face that looked as if he had only just started shaving. From his complexion, he was blond or fair and as he took his hat off it revealed neatly cut blond hair. There was something eager about the look in his blue eyes. This was probably his first murder.

"The body of Carmine Rivers, the singer is in the bushes just around here." Lola pointed.

"Of course, Miss, please show me." There was a touch of condensation in Eades's voice but he was polite and she led him around and pointed.

For a moment he smiled as if this was a joke but she indicated that he looked a little closer and that was when he caught a glimpse of the body. His body stiffened and he knelt down before standing up with a big sigh.

"Wilson call this in, we need SOCO, the coroner, and officers for interviews. Make sure no one leaves the place until we say so."

Lola knew that SOCO was the Scene of Crime Officers and knew that she would now be taken seriously.

Eades turned back to Lola and his demeanor was a lot less friendly. "Miss, I will need to ask you some questions. It would not be easy to find this body unless you knew it was there." His eyes bored into her and she knew he was looking for signs of guilt. Lola kept her calm and was about to explain but he was no longer looking at her.

Eades had put on some gloves and shoe covers and crawled under the huge rhododendron bush to take a better look. He let out a squeal and backed out of the bushes much quicker than he had gone into them.

"There's something in there." His face was white as a sheet.

"Sassy," Lola called, fighting down a chuckle as this was no place for it. However, she imagined getting up close to Sassy beneath the bushes and in deep shadow must have been quite a shock. The man probably thought he'd met a gremlin. "This is Sassy," Lola said as the Frenchie wiggled her way out of the bushes on her belly, with a big smile on her face. "She would be how we found the body, and I believe the murder weapon."

"Murder weapon?" His eyes were wide and he looked a little as if he had never come across such a situation.

"My dog." Lola pointed at Sassy who was now lying on her back with her tongue lolling over her lips as she waved her stubby legs in the air. "Found a knife in a hedge bottom earlier today. I put it in a bag but we thought it was just a hoax from one of my friends."

"Why do you think it was the murder weapon?"

Lola was about to say because it had angry bird blood on it but she stopped herself just in time. "It has, what I think, might be blood on it."

Eades's eyebrows narrowed. "And yet, you didn't report this? Did you touch the knife?"

Lola thought carefully, had she? No, she wouldn't. She knew enough about evidence protection, she was sure she had used the bag Tanya gave her to take the knife from Sassy. However, under the detective's stare, she was starting to doubt herself. "I don't think so. A friend had a bag, I put it in that."

"Watch a few detective shows do we?" he asked.

"I've done a little bit of work with my local police and I'm a private investigator. Even though I didn't think it was anything, I thought it was better to be safe rather than sorry."

"Where is the weapon now?"

There was a definite chill in his voice. Lola swallowed and Sassy jumped to her feet, placed herself between Lola and Eades, and let out a Frenchie scream.

Eades jumped back and an angry expression crossed his face.

The Frenchie scream was enough to make even the toughest amongst us jump and the detective had just had a scare but Lola, once more, had to bite her tongue to keep a straight face.

"Sassy, it's okay, girl," she said.

"The weapon?" Eades said.

"It's in my locker."

"I think we need to talk some more," Eades said and Lola knew that he thought she was the killer.

At that moment, Linc and the rest of the team returned and the detective began to direct them to the body.

"Wilson, take the lady and her friend back to the spa, there is some evidence to collect. See that it is handled properly and then escort these two and hold them until I return." He turned back to Lola. "You have the murder weapon and you found the body. I will be talking to you very soon."

Lola let out a sigh, so much for a relaxing day!

OPEN AND SHUT CASE

"What happened?" Linc asked Lola as they followed Constable Wilson back to the spa.

"He got quite a scare," Lola said.

"Really, I didn't think that would be too bad a scene for a seasoned detective."

Lola couldn't help the chuckle this time. "He crawled into the bushes to come face to face with Sassy in the shadows. I didn't realize she had crawled back under there. His face was as white as a sheet when he bolted out."

Linc chuckled with her and she could see that Wilson was trying to hide his smile. Oh dear, what had she done? The poor detective might never live this down.

When they got back to the spa, Wilson took them around to the front and to the staff entrance. As they came past the car park she could see that police cars had blocked off the entrance and were not letting anyone leave. A few people were peeking out of the windows, but Lola didn't recognize any of them.

Lola wondered how Jinny was taking this and she didn't envy the police's job of interviewing her.

"Through here, please." The constable led them through the spa. "What is the evidence and where is it?"

"I believe it's the murder weapon," Lola said. "Sassy here found it."

"I sniffies it out good." Sassy sat in front of him and he blinked as if he hadn't seen her before.

"Well, aren't you the cutest," he said bending down to scratch her under the chin.

"Me cutest." Sassy sighed and grumbled as he scratched her.

The police officer took a mobile from his pocket and snapped a few pictures. Sassy posed for him, giving him her widest and most gremlin-like grin. Set in stone, she would look perfect on the top of the house.

"It's in my locker," Lola said. "I don't know why I kept it because at the time we thought it was a prank... I guess old habits and all that."

Wilson stood up and smiled. "Lead the way."

Lola walked to the door of the ladies' changing rooms and stopped.

"We need the evidence, Miss, please carry on."

Lola stood back and pointed to the ladies' sign.

The constable turned a bright shade of pink. "Ahh, errm, I... Just a moment." He activated the radio pinned to his jacket. "Could I have a female officer at the east entrance to the ladies' changing rooms please to secure some evidence?"

"On my way."

It was just a minute before a tall, slim uniformed police officer with a big smile, short brown hair, and chocolate brown eyes turned up. "Too afraid to go in, Willy?" she asked.

"It's Wilson, don't call me that," he said but the grin on his face said he probably enjoyed the teasing.

"Well, Miss, I'm Constable Harris. It looks like this is a job for the A team, by that I mean the ladies." She winked at Wilson before pushing open the door.

Lola showed her to her locker all the time looking for her friends but the changing rooms were empty. It looked like the police had already started to move people into controlled areas where they could be interviewed.

Lola crossed to her locker and opened it, she was about to reach in but the PC stopped her. "Let me, I understand how to handle evidence, and the least contamination the better."

Lola nodded and opened the door. There, on a shelf on its own, was the knife, still encased in the bag that Tanya had given her. "That bag had suntan lotion in it... before. I turned it inside out, but just in case there is any residue." Lola shrugged. "It was all I had and we thought it was a hoax. I didn't touch the knife with my bare hands."

"Well done. That's a nasty-looking weapon." She pulled it out and placed it and the bag straight into an evidence bag sealing it, she then let out a whistle. "Expensive too."

"It looks that way."

"If we could find the owner of this, then we would probably have our killer."

For a moment Lola wanted to say nothing but she realized that would not ingratiate her with the police if it later came out that she knew. "I believe it was a gift to the boyfriend, Scott Brussard. I didn't see it close up. I did see Jinny with a knife but it was from a distance. It could have been this one, it might not have been."

Sassy let out a series of grumbles. "It sniffies of Jinny," Lola heard.

"I think Linc, Lincoln, Martin Hall saw Scott with this knife but my gut instinct says he didn't do it."

"Well, that is very interesting, and aren't you the detective." Harris tapped her on the arm. "The thing is, we've already heard that he was dumped by the victim and that always leads to short tempers. These things are usually so much easier than they are on the TV. A young man like that lost not only his booty call but, no doubt, a nice earner. I think this will be an open and shut case."

"It's just that he was not really into her. I think he was just along for the ride... there was no real emotion when it ended."

"You could tell all that could you? Well, maybe we should have you on the force." She chuckled a little and began to walk out of the changing rooms.

"I could tell, man had no lovey luvs," Sassy said.

Wilson and Linc were waiting outside the dressing room. "Take these two to the conservatory. I will take this to the detective and I think we will be coming for Scott. It looks like the dumped man owned the knife."

With a big grin, she turned and walked away.

"Not thinky it was him," Sassy said.

"Neither do I," Lola said out aloud before she realized it.

"What?" Linc said.

Wilson raised an eyebrow.

"I was just positing, I don't think it was Scott."

"I don't know," Linc said. "It would be logical."

Wilson laughed this time. "Leave it to the experts. You folks watch too much CSI and think you know everything."

Lola knew she had no choice but to follow him, but she had the awful feeling that a miscarriage of justice was about to take place. She couldn't allow that, now could she?

LOCKED IN

They were led up to the conservatory. Another uniformed officer was at the doors and he nodded to let them in. "You will be interviewed in due course," Wilson said. "Please don't talk to anyone about what happened."

"Perhaps I can go to find my friends?" Lola asked.

"I'm sorry, if they are not up here then they are in one of the other rooms. I'm sure there's a reason for the segregation." His face said he didn't have a clue and Lola doubted the officers had had the time to think about such things yet. They were merely doing their best to keep control of people and to prevent the perpetrator from leaving.

Wilson held open the door looking very awkward, if she argued with him he would fold but what was the point? Her friends were capable of looking after themselves, now she wished she had picked her mobile up when she visited her locker.

"Please hand over any phones," Wilson said.

Lola shrugged. "I don't have mine."

Linc handed his over reluctantly. "Is this really necessary? I have important calls to make."

"It's just so the killer can't discuss things with any accomplices," Wilson said but he didn't sound convinced. No doubt it was an order from above and he should have said nothing.

"Are we prisoners, are we being locked in?" Linc asked, the expression on his face earnest.

The young PC blushed a lovely crimson and shook his head. "Not at all, sir. We are just asking people to be patient while we investigate the crime. A murder has been committed and we want to make sure that no one else is in danger and that the killer is apprehended."

Linc smiled and Lola realized he had been teasing the officer.

"All right then."

They walked in and Wilson let the doors close behind them.

Lola looked around the room and saw no one she knew well. There were a few people she recognized. Fred, the ginger-headed manager of Carmine was reviewing his papers in the corner. Still in his expensive grey suit, he stood out as everyone else was in a robe. There was no sadness in his stance, but it was possible they hadn't been told yet. If he was the killer he was calm and collected. Lola wasn't sure if he had been fired, if he had quit or if this was just the normal tumultuous relationship between the two.

"Do you have calls to make?" Lola asked, why did that make her suspicious?

"No, I guess I was just pulling his chain. Sometimes I lash out at authority."

Lola could understand that but she continued to glance around the room.

The ex-manager, Matt Wallens was in the opposite corner to Fred, almost as far away from him as he could get. He was also still in his suit, though this one was cream and cheaper and it was harder to spot against the cream robes. Lola was sure the separation was deliberate, the two men despised each other but how did they feel about Carmine?

Matt Wallens', greasy black hair looked even more so and he appeared uncomfortable but not in a guilty way. He looked as if he wanted to be out of there and he kept glancing at Fred.

When Lola thought about it, both men had a motive. They had both been torn down a strip by the singer and had both probably lost out financially. Somehow, Lola didn't think that Carmine endeared much loyalty, except maybe from Alice and Jinny.

The group of girls that Scott had been entertaining were drinking champagne and giggling a lot in a different corner. They could be discounted unless one of them got so angry about the ring tone. Now, wouldn't that be something, stabbed over that annoying tinny song!

Scott was with them and he showed no emotion other than anticipation. He was leaning over a very good-looking girl and whispering into her ear.

There were several other groups of people but Lola couldn't see her friends.

"This way," Sassy said. "I sniffies cake... Moley."

Lola chuckled at Sassy's priorities and wanted to tell her off for using her nickname for Tilly. Luckily, she stopped herself. That would be hard to explain to Linc. When Sassy had first met Tilly, she reminded Sassy of a cartoon mole as she had small round glasses that she peered through with a kind but shrewd look. Sometimes her nose even twitched. The name was not said with malice but it did embarrass Lola.

They set off through the conservatory following Sassy as she trotted at a jaunty pace.

"Why don't we order some drinks?" Linc said pointing at a member of staff who looked to be waiting for just such a request.

Lola could hardly tell him that she knew her friends were on the rooftop because her dog had just told her there was cake. "Let's just check if my group is through here."

"Good idea."

They weaved through the conservatory which was both abuzz with conversation, but there was also an undercurrent of trepidation. Had the police told people why they were being held? They must have, in these days no one would stay without a good reason.

As they walked onto the rooftop, Lola saw her friends at the same table they had used for breakfast. Tilly waved and Alice jumped up and ran over, her orange gown streaming behind her like a cape. For a moment, Lola expected her to take off and fly the short distance. Instead, she ran and pulled Lola into a hug.

"Was it awful?" Alice asked. "We know it would be you who found the body. I'm so sorry, this is all my fault."

Lola hugged her back and pulled away. She was getting better at accepting hugs but still found them a little uncomfortable. When she looked up she could see Sassy sitting in front of Tilly begging for and receiving cake.

"It wasn't too bad. I found Linc and then Sassy just got the scent and led us straight to her."

"Her!" Alice's mouth dropped open as they walked over to the table. "I knew it... was it Carmine?"

"Oh, no, Alice, I'm so sorry," Lola said and pulled her back in for a hug. "I shouldn't have said anything."

Alice slumped down into a chair and the table was a cacophony of questions, flying at Lola from all sides. Lola looked from one to the other but her brain seemed to have stopped functioning.

"Stop, everyone," Tilly said. "Sam, take this." She handed him a £20 note. "Go get us all drinks. Now Lola, what do you know and what can you tell us?"

Lola and Linc walked around the table and took two of the empty chairs. It gave her time to think. The police had told her not to talk to anyone but there was no way she was keeping this quiet and they were not suspects. Her eyes were drawn to Linc, could he be a suspect?

It was possible, but there was nothing she could tell anyone that he didn't already know. He had, after all, been there when she found the body.

For a moment her brain started to go through the suspect list, there were many. Scott would be first but she didn't think it was him. Then there was Jinny, again her instincts said no. The manager, the ex-husband, the old manager, the people who had come and gone from the room. It was a long list.

Linc was also on it as he had the skills and he had had the opportunity, what could be his motive? Though she hated to think of it, could he be a gun, or in this case, a knife for hire?

ON THE CASE

"What have they told you?" Lola asked, thinking this was the safest route.

Talking started all around the table, everyone at once.

Tilly, let out a deafening whistle. "Let me, now, we have been told that a body has been found. We were then escorted here and other people to different rooms and asked to not talk to people about it and to be patient. We were told that we would be interviewed in time."

"Did they take your phones?" Lola asked.

"No, but they took them from some people," Tilly said. "I think people who knew Carmine... I guess it was her that you found?"

Lola nodded. "I can't tell you much more, just that Sassy sniffied..." Lola couldn't believe she had just used the Frenchie's word for sniffing. What would people think? "... Out the body and led us to her. It was well hidden."

"Was it awful?" Alice asked, there was moisture in her eyes. "Such a sad end for Carmine."

"She looked very peaceful," Lola said, though she knew this meant nothing. She hoped that it would ease Alice's pain a little.

"Do they have any suspects?" Sam asked. "Maybe I could help."

Lola liked the fact that he was so keen but he was still doing his training and had some time to go before he would be a police officer. Even if he was, an outside force would not trust him. "I doubt they will want our help, they think it is Scott."

"Well, the way you said that, you don't." Tilly's voice was a little harsh, her shoulders were back, her head high and her expression wary. She had not been impressed with Scott, that much was sure. "Surely, the man was dumped and he went straight to those girls!"

"It could be him but I don't think he had... how can I put it... that much skin in the game."

"I agree," Tanya said. "He was just along for the ride and he knew it was going to end, whether by him or her, I don't think he cared."

"The murder weapon was his," Linc said.

Lola wanted to kick him, her friends probably already knew this but she was trying not to say too much.

"Oh, that knife you found!" Alice's mouth was open wide just as Sam came back with a tray of hot drinks, a big jug of orange juice, a bottle of champagne, glasses, and a plate of chocolates. He handed Tilly the money back. "It was on the house so I thought I'd get plenty to keep us going. Who knows how long we will be here."

NO TIME TO RELAX

Lola took a big gulp of her coffee and leaned back to relax. This day had certainly not turned out as she expected.

"Have a chocolate." Alice pushed the plate in front of her.

Lola looked up to see that her eyes were moist but there was a smile on her face. Alice would battle through anything and Lola had to admire her for her stoicism. Sassy sat on Lola's knee and her nose drifted toward the plate.

"Not for you, little one," Lola said and almost instantly, Linc passed over a piece of cake. Sassy took it gently and jumped off Lola's knee to take it beneath the table to devour.

"She is such a sweetie," Linc said.

Lola took a chocolate. "Are you okay?" she asked Alice.

"Of course, it's sad but I didn't really know her. I guess in some ways I'm part of her story now."

Lola nodded, that was one way of looking at it.

Sam and Louisa had poured themselves a glass of champagne and though they still looked happy they were a little less exuberant. Tanya kept checking her watch. "I called Wayne, he is going to see if he can get us cleared out of here."

"Don't!" Lola almost snapped the word. "Sorry, I just would like to stay as long as possible and interview a few people. I'm just giving it a moment and then going to talk to Scott."

"Oh, of course." Tanya started tapping into her phone. "I'll tell him to leave it alone."

"A moment?" Tilly raised her eyebrows.

"I need to decide what to tell him and how to approach it. I must be careful that I don't help anyone have an alibi or give them information that could change their testimony but I don't think he did it. Look at him."

They all turned and looked across and into the conservatory. Scott was draped over the blonde laughing and behaving in a most relaxed manner.

"He certainly doesn't look guilty," Alice said, "unlike Fred. Look at him, he looks like he's counting her money."

"Why would he be doing that?" Lola asked. "He probably doesn't know she's dead and even if he did, how much money was there?"

"He knows if he killed her," Alice said.

Fred was pouring over papers scribbling here and there. He pushed one lot away, grabbed a tablet, and began tapping furiously on the screen.

"Remember Elvis," Alice said.

Lola nodded but she didn't quite see the relevance.

Alice shook her head. "You're usually quicker than this. When a singer dies they hit the charts. I realize that Carmine will not reach the heady heights of Elvis but it could be a motive."

Lola nodded, could it? Would her death cause her songs to hit the charts? It was possible and was worth thinking about. Suddenly, she wanted to see what Fred was working on, but how?

"Let's go talk to him," Alice said and stood up, her arms folded across the florescent robe, her face firm. Just for a moment, she reminded Lola of a prize fighter, squaring up in the ring. Alice was certainly ready for a showdown.

"Let me handle this," Lola said.

"I will know what to ask."

"Yes, you would, but you might be a little too invested in this, emotionally."

Tilly pulled Alice's robe causing her to sit back in her seat. "Lola's right, let her do this and know that your knowledge was what lead her to the killer.

Lola gulped. Poor Fred had already been convicted just for making a few notes. "Let's see what he's up to first."

Lola took a last drink of her coffee and stood up. "I'll come with you," Linc said.

"Me too!" Sassy was already at her side.

"I'll take you," Lola said to Sassy and chuckles went around the table, "but, I might be better solo on this one." Lola smiled at Linc and he sat back down.

She knew her friends were going to tell him that she was a crazy lady who spoke to her dog, but it didn't matter. She had a crime to solve and one very credible suspect.

Lola strolled casually into the conservatory, Scott was still entertaining the young woman but his eyes drifted across to her. He was aware of what was going on, was that suspicious?

It could be, but most people in here must wonder why they had been herded into the conservatory and plied with drinks.

"Mr. Stilby," Lola said as she put on her most endearing smile and hoped she didn't look like a mad woman, who had been dragged through a hedge backward that was grimacing at him. "We met earlier, how are you?"

Apparently, she didn't look too bad as his eyes traveled down to the opening of her robe and then back to her face. Charming!

"Please, take a seat." He indicated.

"My friend is a big fan of Carmine's, a really big fan and she asked if I could get a little insight into her manager. We all know that you are the force behind her." Lola knew that a man like this would love to have his ego stroked.

"Yes, a singer is nothing without a good manager."

"Can you let us know what you are planning?" Lola reached across the table and with a cheeky grin she took his tablet.

He smiled and tried to pull it back but Lola held firm.

On the screen was a list, Celebrity Escape, the reality TV show was on the top, followed by a bunch of other promotion ideas. Lola let him have the tablet back. He couldn't be the killer as he was planning appearances for Carmine. Somehow, she didn't think he knew his client too well. No way would Carmine go on that show.

Lola was back to square one. She looked across at her friends, Linc was watching her like a hawk. Could it be him?

"Maybe, you would like a drink?" Fred asked. "Later, once they have allowed us out of here, I could show you some memorabilia that I have in my room and we could share a bottle of bubbly." He licked his lips in anticipation.

Lola couldn't believe he was doing this. The last time they had met he had almost pushed her into the bushes and he didn't even remember the hard stare she had given him.

"Thanks, but I'm not sure I'll have the time."

"Well, your loss." Realizing that he had struck out he put his attention back on the tablet.

Lola stood and glanced across at Scott. He looked busy but she decided to go over anyway.

"Does anyone know what's going on?" Lola asked as she walked over to the group.

The girls were giggling and it was obvious that their idea of a spa day was to consume large amounts of alcohol and have a good time. Lola couldn't blame them.

"I heard a body has been found." A brunette that was two down from Scott said. "And that he was stabbed with a vicious-looking knife."

"What!" Scott turned to them and reached for his robe. For a moment he patted the pockets and a look of panic came over his face. Then his eyes flicked over to the table next to the room he had been dumped from.

"Really?" Lola asked. "How did you hear that?"

"I was in the ladies' and the police were talking. They didn't realize I was there so I kept quiet. They said it was some man, Rhodesian I think."

"Isn't that a type of dog?" a lady with a short black pixie cut said.

"I think it's a country too," another added.

Lola had to bite her tongue. The suspect would be some man, and the body was found in the Rhododendrons. Of course, the girls had been drinking heavily all day. Scott looked a lot more relaxed, had he expected Carmine to be dead? The knife had certainly upset him.

"Oh, my goodness, why didn't you tell us?" The girl next to her said. "We could be locked in here with a killer."

"No, I'm sure the police know who it is. I heard they took the cell phones off some people. No doubt, those are their suspects," Lola said and she noticed that Scott's face blanched a little.

"Of course, of course," The woman that Scott was with said. "They would keep the dangerous ones in a different area."

"That's possible," Lola said, "but they probably kept most people where they were. In my experience, they will deal with the scene first and then come and talk to the suspects."

"Really," the blonde said. "You have experience."

"I do, I'm a private investigator and I've helped the police on numerous murder cases. Well, actually, I've helped those who were wrongly arrested beat a murder charge."

"Me too," Sassy said and all eyes dropped to her. "They understood me." Sassy gave a little Frenchie scream and chased her tail for 2 complete circuits before dropping to the tiled floor.

"Oh, my, that is just the cutest little doggy." The blonde got up out of her seat and crawled on her knees across to Sassy. Sassy crawled into the woman's lap and rolled over onto her back for a belly rub.

"Speak of the devil," Lola said. "It looks like they are coming for someone, right now."

All eyes turned to the door where DS Eades and PC Wilson were coming into the conservatory.

Scott turned an even whiter shade of pale and Lola heard him gulp. Eades's eyes were firmly on Scott and he looked like a man on a mission.

CUFFED OR NEARLY

Eades arrived in front of them with PC Wilson almost having to jog to keep up.

"Miss Ramsay," he said. "What a coincidence that you are talking to our number one suspect." He pulled a notebook out of his pocket and made a big display of opening it.

"Really," Lola said. "I was just saying hello."

"Well, I hope you haven't been informing them of what is happening. That could be considered obstructing justice."

Sassy jumped off the blonde's lab and leaped at Eades, her teeth snapping. Oh, no! The little dog had learned a trick recently when she was after a very evil man. Biting him in a delicate place, she had forced him back over a railing and into some water. Though Eades was annoying her, the last thing Lola needed was the Frenchie hanging onto the front of his trousers.

Eades jumped back as fear marred his face.

"Sassy, don't upset the nice detective anymore." Lola turned to Eades. "I do hope she didn't give you too much of a scare."

Wilson was chuckling but Lola knew that she should shut up. The last thing she needed to do was embarrass the man even more.

"I've had much worse than seeing a rat under some bushes."

Sassy jumped, snapping her teeth once more before sitting down in front of him with the cutest expression she could muster.

"Please control your dog, what is it doing in here, anyway?"

"She's my service dog," Lola said.

Eades raised an eyebrow, for a moment Lola thought he would take it further but he let out a sigh that spoke of exhaustion and Lola felt a little guilty. The man had done her no harm and looked as if he had been working too hard and too long.

"If I can help at all," Lola said, "please ask."

Eades nodded and his features relaxed, he took the words in the spirit of apology that they had been meant.

"Now, I would like to talk to you, Scott Brussard, is it?"

Scott nodded. "May I ask why?"

"I believe you were... shall we say... dating, one Carmine Rivers." Eades was watching Scott intensely. Looking for any micro expressions that might cross his features. Lola was doing the same and the man was either very good or he didn't know.

Scott shrugged. "Not anymore, she gave me the push earlier because she heard me say a few ungentlemanly things."

"How did that make you feel?"

"I've been expecting it for a while. The woman's desperate, but I swear it was always consensual, no matter what she says. I kept forgetting our 30-day anniversary and then our 40th and so on and so forth, it was getting exhausting."

"How much money did she give you?" Eades asked.

Scott snarled. "Not enough."

"Is that why you killed her?"

Scott's mouth dropped open. "Killed, Carmine's dead?"

"That's correct." Eades was not quite as good at controlling his expressions for the disappointment in Scott's reaction was plainly written on his face.

"As well as the Rhodesian man?" the brunette who had been in the ladies' earlier asked.

Eades glanced at Lola. "What have you been telling them?"

Lola shook her head. "It wasn't me."

"That was me," the brunette said. "I heard the copper's talking about it, how they had found a Rhodesian man dead. Well, I think that's what they said."

Eades's pen was paused over his notebook and the confusion was clear on his face.

"I believe the lady, who has had a few glasses of champagne, may have heard rhododendron."

"That was it," she said with a look of triumph on her face. "The murdered man was a Rhododendron."

A few of the girls burst out laughing and Scott's face crumpled as it dawned on him that he was the main suspect in Carmine's murder. Once more his hands patted his robe.

"What is it you're looking for?" Eades asked. "The murder weapon, by any chance?"

"I... I... Carmine gave me a knife. I thought I had it but maybe I left it when she dumped me."

"Did she ask for it back?" The detective's eyes were boring into Scott.

"I... I... no, she didn't."

"So you kept it and have since misplaced it?" The look on Eades's face was one that bordered on triumph.

"I guess, but I could have left it... yes, that's it... I left it at the pool after... well. Then Jinny put it outside the room. She told me to take it but Carmine kept me waiting, and I forgot."

Eades smiled again. It was a smile to put the suspect at ease. One that said, I hear you, I understand, but Lola knew it was all for show. To lull Scott into a false sense of security. "That must have been quite humiliating? Sitting there with everyone knowing you were about to be dumped. I imagine that would make me very angry."

"Nah, not really. In some ways, it was a relief. I mean, don't get me wrong, Carmine was all right... but..." Scott let his eyes travel around the group of women, lingering on each of them, including Lola. "As you can imagine, if I compared her to these lovely ladies... well... it gave me itchy feet."

"That makes a lot of sense. Can I ask where you were around..." Eades skipped back through his notebook. "Between 12 and 2 pm?"

Scott smiled. "I was with these lovely ladies."

"Not all of it," pixie cut said. "You went off to the gents' and you were gone a good thirty minutes."

"What time was that?" Eades asked.

"After lunch and before cocktails, who wears a watch on a spa day?"

Eades indicated to Wilson and the young PC pulled his handcuffs off his belt.

"Scott Brussard, I would like you to accompany me to the station where you will be questioned further about this."

"Why, why would I kill her?" Scott asked and he turned to Lola. "Can you help me?"

"No, she can't," Eades said, "and the why is easy. She came after you. Either she didn't want to let you go or she wanted her money back and you lost your temper. Maybe she even wanted that fancy knife back and you gave it to her."

He nodded at PC Wilson once more.

Lola looked long and hard at Scott and she was sure he was innocent but what could she do?

CHANGE OF HEART

PC Wilson was trying to get through the drunken group of women to slap the handcuffs on Scott. Sassy was in front of the blonde on the floor and the other women seemed incapable of moving.

Eades shook his head. “Get on with it man.”

“But, Serg, they… I…”

“You!” Scott was looking at Lola. “Will you help me? I’ll hire you but I swear I didn’t do this.”

Lola nodded. “DS Eades, may I have a word?”

He shrugged. “Take 5 Wilson but make sure he doesn’t give us the slip.” Eades moved his head to indicate for Lola to follow him and they walked away to a quiet area of the conservatory. Sassy followed and Lola noticed that Eades actually smiled at her.

"I'm so sorry about Sassy," she said.

"You said she was your service dog, may I ask in what capacity?"

Lola wondered whether to say for anxiety or to mention PTSD. In the end, she decided that the full truth would be the best course. "I was in Afghanistan, I can suffer from PTSD, she helps me through the attacks and she can spot when one is coming on and usually stop it."

"That's impressive," he said. "You said she led you to the body, but you couldn't see it under there so how did you know to look? If my dog was sniffing in the bushes I would imagine it would be after cat poop."

"I told her," Sassy said and Eades looked down at her as she grumbled.

"She makes some funny noises," he said.

"Look who's talking," Sassy said and sat on her butt, back legs out, bottom lip protruding.

"I've done some scent work with her, she indicates different scents with different poses."

"Must have been quite a course to have had bodies on it," he said.

"I guess I was a little more inclined to look having found the knife earlier."

He nodded, it was a plausible explanation. "What did you want?"

"I don't think that Scott is your killer, if you take him away then you will soon have to release everyone from the spa and that could let the real killer go. Hold him here, talk to him but let me see what I can find out from him for you."

"Scott has a motive, the murder weapon is his, and I guarantee his fingerprints will be on it. He has search and rescue experience so he would know how to hide a body and he looks like he could be capable, in my eyes he is the perfect suspect."

"But what does your gut say?" Lola asked.

Eades shook his head and for a moment she thought she had lost him but then he stopped, his back to her. He was very still for a few moments and she held her breath. Then he turned back and he smiled. "My gut says it's too easy. Now, my boss would kill me for that. He's always saying this is real life and in real life, it is usually really easy. People mainly kill for passion or money. That passion can be love, hate, jealousy, humiliation, anger you name it but it is usually the person you expect it to be... and yet, I agree with you. This guy didn't have a passion for her, I can see it in his eyes. He doesn't even feel humiliated."

Eades scratched his head.

"Are you agreeing with me?"

"Yeah, for now, I will hold him here. You can talk to him and I will interview people and let them go one by one, but if we haven't found a better suspect by 7 pm when most of these people will be leaving, then I take him in."

"Thanks."

"Don't thank me yet, you just rose onto the top of my suspect list."

Lola gulped, what had she done?

* * *

"Right," Eades said to Wilson," Where is Jinny?"

"She's in the manager's office upstairs." Wilson's face looked like he had seen a ghost. "Don't look so worried, Constable, I'm not going to make you comfort her again."

"Thank you, sir."

"I want you to stay on the doors up here and make sure this lot stays calm. They can have drinks and food but they can't leave. There are toilets just outside so they can visit but you stay near so they can't sneak off, are we clear?"

Wilson nodded.

"Miss Ramsay, you're with me."

Lola smiled across at Scott and saw him relax. "Call me Lola," she said to Eades as he led the way out of the conservatory.

"Miss Ramsay is fine for now."

Lola rolled her eyes without letting him see, it was like that, was it?

They walked along the corridor past the dining rooms and back to the stairs, this time he took a barrier down from the flight leading up and indicated for her to enter.

Lola walked up the next flight of stairs onto the next level. The layout was very similar but the landing was empty. A corridor led off to the left and he went to the first door, where a uniformed officer stood outside.

"How is she?" Eades asked.

It was Constable Harris... she grimaced. "Quieter, for now."

"That's something." Eades knocked and entered the room. Jinny was seated on a small damson-colored leather chesterfield sofa in a corner of the office. The room was beautifully furnished with the seating area having two matching chairs and a glass coffee table. Across from it was a large mahogany desk and the walls were lined with shelves holding books of all shapes and colors.

Jinny rose to her feet. "Have you found who did this? Was it Scott?"

"We're still investigating," Eades said. "I need to ask Miss Ramsay a few questions, why don't you let Constable Harris take you for a cup of tea?"

"No, no, no, you won't push me out of this," her voice had risen to the heights of hysteria.

Eades was looking decidedly panicked. No doubt he could deal with a hardened criminal but the desperate tears of a woman who had lost so much was too much for him to handle. It was at that moment that Lola realized something about Jinny. Did it change things? Did it make her a suspect? It would certainly explain why she had put up with so much, and why she was so devastated. Did it also give her a motive?

JINNY'S SECRET

"Let me handle this," Lola whispered to Eades over Jinny's wailing and desperate sobs.

The look of relief on his face was immense.

"Jinny, don't worry, we are not going to cut you out of this. There is so much you can tell us. I'm sure your knowledge will help us find Carmine's killer. I'm truly sorry for your loss, please, sit down and help us."

Jinny's shrieking stopped and she grabbed a handkerchief from the box on the coffee table and noisily blew her nose. Tossing that into the bin she grabbed another and tried to blot the tears that were streaming down her face. It was to no avail, the moment she blotted some, more flooded down her cheeks.

"Would you like a nice cup of tea?" Lola asked, knowing that is what Tilly would ask.

Jinny looked up and sank back down onto the sofa. "Please."

"Harris," Eades said and the PC left closing the door behind her.

"Tell me all about Carmine," Lola said, she leaned forward to show that she was eager to hear it.

Jinny patted at her tears and sat back. At first, she couldn't speak, the words were just too raw and wouldn't come. Then a slight smile crossed her face. "She was wonderful, so much better than anyone ever knew." A bout of sobs turned her words into an incoherent mumble.

"What did you say?" Eades asked and Lola glared at him. He shook his head and waved his hands for her to continue.

Sassy growled at Eades before going over to Jinny and leaning against her leg. The distraught woman began to stroke the dog without even realizing she was doing it.

"My friend, Alice, was a big fan of Carmine's," Lola said. "She told me all about Carmine's amazing talents."

"Oh, yes, such an amazing talent. People thought she was difficult... she wasn't... she just wanted everything to be right, the art was everything to her. So many people nowadays want to compromise. They think good enough is good enough and yet you can always do better and that was what Carmine Believed."

PC Harris arrived with a tray of drinks.

"Thank you," Eades said and Jinny jumped a little. It was as if she had forgotten he was there.

Lola poured the tea for her and Jinny. There was a coffee for Eades, Harris obviously knew him well.

With all these drinks, Lola hoped she wouldn't have to leave the interview at a delicate stage. Today seemed to be almost one drink leading to another and her bladder was not as good as it used to be.

Lola handed the cup over to Jinny and received a smile in reply. "Take your time and tell us who you think could have done this."

Eades leaned forward a little.

"I think it was Scott," Jinny said. "After all, he had just been dumped and it was his knife."

"After he... was dumped... did he leave the knife... in the pool room?" Lola asked.

Jinny nodded. "I then put it near the office, in a bag."

"So he left it?" Eades asked.

Jinny patted at a new batch of tears and nodded. "I took so much time finding the perfect gift and he just left it like it was nothing. If Carmine had ever given me such a precious thing I would have treasured it... forever."

"So, who had the knife?" Eades asked.

"I left it on the table next to the room in a plastic bag. I pointed it out to Scott, I thought he, Scott, might take it... as a memento of their time together."

"When was the last time you saw it?" Lola asked.

Jinny dropped her head, taking a moment to think. "The bag was still there the last time I was up in the conservatory."

"Who could have taken it?" Eades asked, he had that look, the one Lola recognized. He smelt a vital piece of information and he was excited to hear it. It meant that his senses were heightened as he wanted to take in every aspect of the person's demeanor, to make sure that he got it all.

"Anyone, most of the people I invited up to see Carmine sat there, and then there were all the people in the spa. I never kept my eye on it as I was so angry. It was not cheap and... oh, anyone could have taken it."

Eades deflated, like a helium balloon.

"Do you have a list of them all?" Lola asked. "All the people who came to see Carmine?"

"Yes, I can go through them one by one. But I still think it was Scott. Passions run high and to lose someone like Carmine, well, that would be such a blow. The man was always arrogant and he likes to hunt. He would know how to do such an evil thing."

"It's possible, but I don't think so and he has an alibi." Lola noticed that Eades raised an eyebrow and she gave him a look that said, run with me on this.

Eades nodded.

Scott's alibi was weak but Lola needed Jinny to look beyond him.

For the next 20 minutes, Jinny told them of the people who had been interviewed or upset by Carmine that day. There was the ex-boyfriend who kept asking Carmine to stop following him, the husband who thought she was going to accuse him of abuse, the two managers, one who had lost his job and the other who might, and three backing singers who had problems with their contracts, and an accountant who Carmine had accused of cheating her. They all had equally good reasons for killing Carmine. With each new name, Jinny was sure that this was the killer. Lola tried to keep it all in her mind, while Sassy was leaning against Jinny's leg offering comfort.

"I think we have a lot of suspects," Eades said, "Maybe we should leave Miss Peppers to rest, for now."

"Of course," Lola said. "Jinny, Carmine liked to have a man in her life, a strong man, one who challenged her, didn't she?"

Jinny nodded.

"How did you feel about the men she chose?"

Jinny's face changed, there was a touch of red on her cheeks and real anger in her eyes. "They didn't deserve her. None of them loved her as I did. None of them treasured her or treated her with respect. They used her and threw her away when things got rough. That is not a relationship. Real love is about working through the hard times as much as the good ones. About being there and supporting the one you love. Loyalty is paramount and support should be both ways."

"You gave her that loyalty, that support, didn't you?" Lola said the words quietly, she wanted to coax this out of Jinny in the most pleasant way possible.

"I did, I loved her..."

"Did she ever reciprocate that love?" Lola asked.

Jinny stared over Lola's head for a moment, as if she was making a momentous decision. "No, she only liked men."

Eades gasped.

"I could have been everything for her if she would have just given me a chance."

"You... loved her?" Eades asked.

Jinny nodded. "There, I said it. I loved her from the bottom of my heart. I wanted her to be mine." Jinny had squared her shoulders and her expression was one of pride and defiance. It was as if she was expecting them to challenge her.

"But she didn't return your love did she?"

"No... she did appreciate me... sometimes."

"But she didn't return your love in the way you needed her to, did she?" Eades pressed.

Jinny shook her head. "I would have given her everything. I gave her my heart and she..."

"Threw it back at you," Eades said.

"She only liked men."

"How did that make you feel?" Eades asked as once more, excitement lit up his face.

"Awful." Jinny began to sob once more.

Oh, dear, it looked like they had another suspect.

"DS Eades," Harris put her head around the door. "There is trouble in the relaxation room."

NO TIME TO RELAX

Eades face morphed from exhaustion to confusion. Lola guessed that the detective was struggling with the oxymoron of the two terms, trouble in the relaxation room. He was clearly confused!

"Okay, Jinny, we might have more questions later, but for now stay here... I hope you feel better soon." The man shook his head, he really didn't know how to speak to a distraught woman.

Lola reached across and squeezed Jinny's hands. "I will be back later if you need to talk."

Sassy rubbed against Jinny's leg once more and then followed Lola out of the room.

"Not her," Sassy said.

"How do you know?" Lola answered without thinking.

"Know what?" Eades asked.

This was the last thing Lola needed, and she almost said, sorry, I was just answering my dog! "Sorry, I was just thinking it wasn't her and asking myself the question. I guess the words came out without me thinking."

Lola could hear Sassy chuckling. "She sniffies not like a killer. Thinking sad, angry, regret but not guilty."

"I tend to agree with you," Eades said and then turned to Harris. "Right, what's the trouble?" Eades ran a hand through his short salt and pepper hair.

"A man is causing quite a stink. I said we are on our way," Harris was striding out along the corridor and practically ran down the stairs. She stepped over the rope barrier before removing it for them. They turned right and then left and down another flight of stairs. Harris weaved through the corridors without hesitation, and as they got closer the muffled sound of shouting came to them.

"We still have to consider Jinny as a suspect, I feel like you but it's not enough," Eades said as they raced along to keep up with PC Harris.

"I guess she has a motive, but I don't think it was her," Lola said.

"My gut agrees with you but logically, I'm not so sure. She was spurned and from what I've heard treated pretty badly by the woman she loved." Eades's face turned a little pink. He seemed uncomfortable with the subject.

Lola smiled. "Yes, that's true but I'm sure it was not the first time. I get the feeling Jinny is a bit of a Pollyanna."

"A what!"

"Optimistic."

"Oh, yeah, she would have to be." Eades shook his head as the shouting got louder.

"Let me go, I have things to do."

They rounded the corner to see Bruce Powell squaring up to two uniformed PCs.

"What's going on here?" Eades barked and the men all pulled apart. It was like school boys scattering at the sound of the headmaster's voice.

Bruce recovered first. "I want to go to the gym, I have a session booked with a trainer. It was bad enough that woman followed me here, again, but I paid to use the facilities, not to sit here all day."

The anger fizzled out of him as they got closer. Maybe, it was the stern look on Eades' face. Lola could see that Bruce Powell was in his mid to late 50s. A handsome man, tall, powerfully built. It seemed that Carmine had a type. The men were all like action movie stars. His black hair was thick and a little too black. She suspected it was dyed. Deeply tanned, he looked after himself and appeared a little arrogant and vain. Though he was wearing the same robe as all the day guests were, he wore it with style and Lola saw that he was wearing some form of a medallion. The man was a player.

"What woman would that be?" Eades asked as he guided Bruce back into the relaxation room and over to one corner. "Get me some light on in here, Harris," Eades shouted.

The room was subdued, almost dark. There were over a dozen beds all around the room in little alcoves for people to come in and sleep. Soothing music was just audible and the air was scented with lavender.

The lights came on and Bruce blinked like a bear coming out of hibernation.

"Sit," Eades said pointing at a bed. "Harris, bring me a chair."

Before they could make their way to the bed, Sassy ran around the back of it and then around the room. Running past them at a great speed she leaped at the bed and bounced straight off the other side. She ran around for another pass leaping at the bed from over 6 feet away she landed on it, stopped instantly, and rolled onto her back. As they approached she was waving her legs in the air, her little pink tongue poking out from floppy jowls.

"Needed that, been still too long," Sassy said.

Bruce stared at Sassy and then at Lola. She smiled at him but Eades coughed bringing them all back to the situation at hand. "Sit," he said.

Bruce sat on the bed but there was something stiff about his movement. Had he hurt his back? Could he have done that by hiding a body in the bushes?

Before Eades could do much other than glare at Powell, Harris brought in 2 chairs and set them down in front of the bed. She smiled and left.

Lola took the one on the right and Eades pulled out his notebook and pen and took his time sitting down. Bruce adjusted the belt of his robe, it was a strange gesture, as if the belt was causing him some discomfort but that made no sense as the robes were super soft and comfortable.

"I asked, what woman was following you?" Eades repeated.

"Sorry, I..." His eyes glanced back at Sassy. For now, she was lying on the bed next to him. "It was Carmine Rivers, we split up, so why does she turn up wherever I go?"

"Is that why you killed her?" Eades spoke so matter of factly.

"Well, that's a thought." Bruce stopped and the color seemed to slip off his face as he realized why he was being questioned and why they were being held. "No, no, no... I didn't mean that... is she... dead... really dead?"

"Yes, she really is," Eades noted something in his book, and on the bed, Bruce squirmed. "What were you doing between 10 am and 2 pm?"

"I..." For a moment his mouth fell open and he looked at the door. He reminded Lola of a rabbit caught in the headlights and she had to admit that Eades gave quite a powerful stare when he wanted to.

"Spit it out man," Eades said.

"I was, well, this morning around 10 am I met Carmine in the Zen Garden."

"The what?!" Eades shook his head as if none of this made any sense.

"The Zen Garden, I had gone there to meditate. I had just started chanting and was raising my chakra to the next level when who should appear but Carmine."

"What happened?"

"I told her that I wasn't happy seeing her there and that it was over and that she should leave me alone."

Eades made a note in his book, taking his time. Lola could almost see Bruce squirming and part of her wanted to chuckle. The man was behaving like a naughty schoolboy, but could he be the killer?

"Do you have any witnesses?" Eades asked, closing his notebook as if the question sealed Bruce's fate.

Bruce gulped. "Carmine... well... no, I... no, I don't... but I didn't kill her, I swear."

"Actually," Lola said. "I was a witness, I was on the rooftop garden and I saw a rather heated argument between the two of you." She raised an eyebrow.

Bruce spluttered and then had the good graces to blush. He lowered his head.

"I can confirm that Carmine left relatively unharmed; however, you did shove her twice. And if the pacing is your way of raising your chakra, it didn't look that Zen to me."

"I... I..." Bruce didn't manage to get any more out before he was stopped by Eades.

"He hit her?" Eades asked.

Lola shrugged. "It was physical and out of order but it was more a shove and she was berating him. I'm not excusing it, but it seemed more like a reaction rather than an attack."

Bruce shuffled on the bed. "She wouldn't leave me alone. I asked her to go and she kept getting closer and closer, in the end, I pushed her away. I shouldn't have done it, who knows, it might have even been a ploy to get money out of me. It wouldn't be the first time. Maybe that snake, Jinny, was filming it, and then she could bribe me later."

"That gives you a motive," Eades said. "I think we'd better hear everything you did today, and let's hope, for your sake, that you have an alibi."

Bruce smiled.

Lola watched him closely, was that the face of a guilty man?

THE FACE OF A GUILTY MAN

"Is that the face of a guilty man?" Lola asked as she stared at Bruce. It was a slightly strange question for it was aimed at Sassy.

Bruce shifted on the bed, it was as if he couldn't sit still. He picked at his robe as if he was adjusting it. Such behavior made Lola think that it could be him. People often found it hard to sit still when they were trying to hide something.

"I was asking myself the same thing," Eades said. "You seemed to have a good motive, Mr. Powell. You wanted to be rid of the woman, you were frightened of what she might do to you, frightened that she might destroy your reputation."

"Not sure what a guilty man face is," Sassy said, as with one paw she scratched her ear. It was a bit of avoidance behavior and Lola felt her own guilt kick in for asking such a non-dog-friendly question. The little dog was using the scratch so that she didn't have to think about the question.

"My dog can smell guilt, what do you think Sassy, is he guilty?"

Sassy got up and crossed the bed to Bruce and as she approached him she took in big sniffies.

"Not guilty," Sassy said, she jumped off the bed and came to sit next to Lola.

"She doesn't like your scent, do you have that alibi?"

Nothing could really be read into this, and Sassy's not guilty did not necessarily mean that Bruce was... not guilty. What it meant was that he was not displaying any signs of guilt, i.e. from his body scents she could not discern that he was feeling guilty. Being guilty and feeling guilty were two very different things.

However, Lola trusted Sassy's instincts, she just needed a better way of asking the Frenchie questions.

"Yes, let's check your alibi. What happened after you attacked Carmine?" Eades asked.

"I didn't attack her." Bruce looked miserable. "I swear I didn't kill her but I came here to be alone. I have an audition coming up next week and I needed to prepare... and I wanted privacy to do it. The next thing I know she turns up with her entourage."

"How were you preparing?" Lola asked.

"Don't think it him, smells citrusy," Sassy said and coughed a little as she backed further away from him.

Lola nearly repeated the word, sometimes it was difficult carrying on a secret conversation. Sassy didn't like citrus smells, she found them so strong that they irritated her throat.

"I wanted time to relax and to meditate, time to prepare a scene for the audition." He lowered his head avoiding their eyes, "And just to prepare physically. That was where I went after the meeting with Carmine."

"So you have an alibi," Eades said.

"Carmine and bushes not citrusy." Sassy was pawing at Lola's leg to let her know that she had important information.

"What?" Lola said.

Lola nearly asked how Sassy could tell. The scent of Patchouli had been strong, surely, it had drowned out any other scents. She must remember to ask Sassy later.

"Of course, I went to the treatment center where I booked in for a treatment." Bruce shook his head. "They would know I was there."

There was something about his manner, he was hiding something and once more he shifted on the bed.

"Being snaky now," Sassy said. "I bet even you can sniffy that!"

Snaky was Sassy's way of saying he was deceiving them. Alice had once called a devious man a snake in the grass and had said he was being snaky. Sassy had picked up on the phrase and liked to use it. Lola took in a breath and nodded, letting Sassy think that she could tell such things. Sometimes, she thought it would be wonderful to be able to sniff out other people's emotions but there again, maybe not.

"What is it you're not telling us?" Lola asked.

Bruce raised his head and then shook it. "Nothing, I had a treatment, there's nothing wrong with that." The man seemed nervous, angry almost and he shifted his hips and tugged at his robe around his waist.

"Someone was with you during this treatment?" Eades asked.

"Citrusy hiding sweat and he needs water." Sassy had wandered over and was sniffing Bruce once more.

"What is she doing?" Bruce asked.

"She's trained to detect certain things, including blood. She's very interested in you."

"There's no blood on me." With wide eyes, he shook his head. "I didn't kill her."

"No blood, needs water," Sassy said.

"Why are you dehydrated?"

"Oh," he let out a big breath of air, "you will find out eventually." Bruce looked at Eades. "I need this to be kept quiet."

"That will depend on what it is. Now tell me your alibi or I will be sending you down to the station... at least you will get your wish, you will be out of this room." Eades shrugged.

"I was having a citrus mud wrap. To lose weight. They saw me go into the room."

"Someone was with you all the time?" Eades asked.

"No, because I was trying to keep it quiet and once the wrap was applied, all I did was lie there. The lady in the beauty suite started the treatment but that was it. I was in there for two and a half hours, they saw me leave. After that, I went for lunch and the staff will remember me I'm sure."

"Was there only one entrance to this room?"

The color slipped off Bruce's face once more. "Well, there was another door but I don't even know if it was locked."

"So no alibi," Eades said.

"Yes, ask the staff, maybe I will be on the CCTV."

"Unfortunately, for you, the spa doesn't have much CCTV. For privacy reasons."

"I had no reason to kill her." Bruce let out a sigh and leaned back. "Carmine's a has-been, and bitter, but no one believed her or took much notice of her. Hart was annoyed at the rumors she was spreading, but I don't think even he would kill her. We had all got used to her ways and, sure, I was angry. I pushed her and I'm not proud but I've hardly eaten for a month and I've given up coffee, so it's understandable."

"Really!" Lola said. "Being hungry and giving up your addiction makes it all right to abuse a woman!?"

"That's not what I said. It wasn't abuse... was it?"

Lola stared hard at him.

"I'm sorry, the woman could push anyone's buttons, but I didn't do it." It was as if a light bulb came on in his mind. Shuffling on the bed he pointed at them. "I would look at Matt Wallens. Rumor had it that he was out and that Fred was taking on his role. It was the only job he had left and without it, the man would be in trouble."

Lola believed him on the first one and her gut said he hadn't done this but what was he hiding.

He kept fidgeting and was uncomfortable. Like the Frenchie, was this avoidance behavior? Was he hiding the fact that he was the killer? Maybe the citrus wrap was a way of masking the scent of blood? It could be him and if not, was Matt a good suspect?

WHAT WAS HE HIDING?

"What do you think?" Eades asked as they left the room.

"I don't think it was him." Lola shrugged her shoulders, this was partly her own gut instinct but also came from Sassy's input. The Frenchie didn't think he was at the scene, could she be wrong?

"He was hiding something." Eades checked his notebook.

"Yeah, he couldn't sit still. He reminded me of a schoolboy unable to face the headmaster's gaze.

"Girdle," Sassy said.

Lola nearly burst out laughing and she looked down at Sassy. She could have sworn that the Frenchie was chuckling as she nodded her head.

"That's what he was hiding under his robe. Made him more sweaty and pinched skin gives good sniffies."

"That dog makes some very strange noises," Eades said.

"Me make funny noises!" Sassy sat down facing away from him.

Lola had to find a way to explain what Sassy had said to Eades. My Frenchie says the man is wearing a girdle, didn't seem like a good option! "I think he is too worried about his own career and his weight. The way he kept shifting? It was almost as if he was uncomfortable."

"That's what made me think it was him, that shifty behavior, being unable to sit still, unable to hold eye contact." Eades was still checking his notes.

"I think... I think he was wearing a girdle, I think that was why he couldn't sit still. He kept pulling at his belt as if it was too tight."

Eades stopped and looked at her. "Really! No, that is too much... why?"

"If he has an audition, then he needs to lose weight and maybe..."

"No... I can't believe Bruce Powell would be wearing a girdle! I saw the man in Mobsters Stand, he was terrific."

Lola shrugged. "The way he was shifting, I would love to see what he has on under his robe."

Sassy snorted.

"I... I didn't mean it like that." Lola pushed a lock of hair off her face and tried to hide the blush that was heating her cheeks.

Eades laughed. "I don't believe this for one moment but I'm mighty curious as to why he was shifting about so much... wait here." Eades turned and went back into the room.

Lola picked Sassy up. "How could you tell that there was no citrus at the murder scene with the strong smell of Patchouli?"

Sassy shook her head and yawned, another way to say that she didn't understand the question.

"The strong smell, did it cover all the other sniffies?" Lola used Sassy's own wording making the conversation as simple as she could.

"You silly. Each sniffy is unique."

Lola kissed Sassy's forehead and put her down. It didn't seem possible to her that Sassy could smell anything over the patchouli but she had once been told that a dog's nose was much more sensitive than our eyes. If we saw a bright color, something fluorescent even, it didn't stop us from seeing other colors. She guessed there was a lot to learn about how dogs detect scent but, on this, Sassy was never wrong. Then she thought about it some more, of course, if a light was too bright it would prevent us from seeing. Could the scent have done that?

Eades came back with a smile on his face. "You were right. He's wearing a back support belt. According to him, it's a medical device. It didn't look like the back support belts I've seen, it looked remarkably like a girdle."

"Do you know anything about this Matt Wallens?" Eades asked having already moved on to his next suspect.

"He is the digital production manager and rumor has it that he was being fired and that Fred Stilby would be taking over his role."

"You seem to know an awful lot about these people. How come?" Eades had casually asked the question but his eyes were keen. It looked like she was back on his suspect list.

"My friend, Alice Beecham is a big fan of Carmine's. She has been giving us a running commentary on all the comings and goings."

"Comings and goings?"

"Let's just say that Carmine didn't make a lot of friends. One moment she could be nice and friendly, the next she would put you down like a bug under her foot. There has been a stream of people going in and out of the room off the conservatory and most of them didn't look happy."

"These people?" He pulled a list out of his pockets.

"I think so, I don't recognize all the names but I have to admit sometimes I miss what Alice is saying. Is that the list Jinny gave you?"

"Yes. I didn't realize that there was upset with more than the boyfriend though."

"I would say almost everyone she met would have their buttons pushed." Lola shrugged.

"Just my luck, a complicated case."

"If you want any background information on these people Alice is the one to ask. However, she is not a suspect."

Eades chuckled. "I'm supposed to be the one who decides that."

They made their way back to the conservatory and walked through it to the room that Carmine had used. Wilson was with them.

"Has this room been processed?" Eades asked.

"Yes, they didn't really find anything."

Eades raised an eyebrow. "That was quick for them to process all that evidence."

Wilson colored. "Sorry... I meant... there was nothing like blood or a weapon."

"Don't worry, lad, I'm only pulling your chain." Eades stepped back into the conservatory and looked at the seat outside with the coffee table next to it. Sure enough, there was a carrier bag on the table.

"Have that carrier checked into evidence. I want it fingerprinted," Eades said.

Wilson nodded and wandered off to get an evidence bag.

"I'll fetch Matt, you may as well sit in, your knowledge is proving useful," Eades said and he set off across the conservatory.

"Sassy, check that bag, can you tell me who touched it?"

Sassy sniffed the bag and then sat down in front of Lola. "Jinny, Scott, Greasy man, 3 women."

"They all touched the bag?"

"Yes."

Lola wanted to ask who the greasy man was but it was too late as Eades escorted Matt into the room and indicated for her to follow him.

With the door closed, they sat behind the desk and Matt sat in front. He looked uncomfortable and was sweating a little. He ran a hand through his greasy hair and moved it back from his face.

"How was your relationship with Carmine?" Eades asked.

"The same as normal, she would shout and threaten to sack me, and then we would be best friends again."

"That must have made you angry, was it worth it? Was she making much money?" Eades grinned, allowing Matt to feel he was just asking questions and not that he was hanging on every word and every nuance of body language.

"It's like anything, some days it didn't feel worth it but you have to look for the future."

That was curious, did Carmine have a future, was there a comeback planned? Somehow Lola couldn't see it. The ideas that Fred had given were great. Going on one of the celebrity TV shows could really have brought her back into the public's eye but she was too belligerent to even consider them. So why was Matt looking to the future?

Did he know something they didn't?

ALIBI

"What future did you see?" Lola asked.

For a moment Matt looked shocked but he hid it quickly. "Singers' careers come and go. Fred and I were working on some ideas to put Carmine back into the spotlight. She was a good singer and given the right promotion she could do well again."

"Was!" Eades said. "What do you mean by that?" The DS looked like the cat covered in cream.

"Do you think you could keep it quiet? Everyone knows that someone was found dead. Most believe it was Carmine, now you are asking me questions about her... it's not rocket science."

"You don't seem too upset." Lola said.

"He not upset, he happy," Sassy said.

"Sorry, Luv, but big boys don't cry."

Eades chuckled. "No, they don't, but they usually show some sign of grief, why is it that you are not at all bothered by her death?"

Matt let out a big sigh. "Okay, you got me. I was totally fed up with the life. I was hardly getting anything from her. I get 10%, well, 10% of nothing is not a lot! And for that, I had to be at her beck and call all the time. I don't need the money and I wanted out of the job. There, I'm not glad she's dead but I'm glad I'm out of it."

"The way I heard it she fired you and you didn't look too happy about it." Lola raised her eyebrows.

Matt chuckled again and folded his arms in front of him. "You don't know Carmine as I do. I wanted out and this was my way. If she thought I wanted to go, she would never let me go even if she wanted me gone. I had to let her think I was desperate for this job and that way she got rid of me. Usually, when she changed her mind I came back, but this time I wasn't going to."

"We will have to see if you have an alibi, but if it wasn't you, who do you think had a reason to kill her?"

"It will be that boyfriend of hers, he attacked Hart with a knife... was Carmine stabbed by any chance?"

Eades looked at Lola. "Did you know about this?"

"It wasn't an unprovoked attack, in fact, the way Scott handled himself would make me more likely to believe his innocence," Lola said.

"What!" Matt laughed. "He slashed at the man with that hunting knife and you had to stop him.

"Tell me about it," Eades said.

Lola sighed but she should have known this would come out. "Ok, Hart Bowers, Carmine's ex-husband was worried that she was going to publicly say he had hit her. Hart asked Scott for help and asked how he felt about Carmine. Scott called her a dried-up old prune and Hart punched him. Scott slashed at him and Hart fell over, Scott looked as if he was going to stab him and I intervened but when I grabbed his arm there was no force in the blow. He was just frightening the man. If he had been angry, an out-of-control person, I would not have been able to stop him so quickly."

"We will talk about this more later. I hear you but that was still an attack with a knife in public." Eades turned back to Matt. "Now, what were you doing between 10 and 1 pm?"

Matt smiled. "Lucky me, I have a solid alibi for all that time. I was in the conservatory for some of it. I then had a meeting with Carmine, Fred, Marilee, Sue, and Becki at the stone circle on the north side of the venue. That had to be around 11.30 and ended... just before 12.30. Carmine was still there with Fred, I think. After that, Marilee and I discussed her contract. I was hoping to help her get out of it as she wished to retire."

"Who are all those people?" Eades asked and then shook his head as he had recognized them on the list.

"Is she really dead?" Matt asked.

There was a touch of grief on his face but it didn't seem genuine. Lola looked down at Sassy and wanted to ask if the grief was real. Sassy caught her eye and understood, she took in a great big sniff.

Lola watched Eades close his notebook. He had discounted Matt as a suspect, had she?

"He's hiding something. Sniffies like me when I take sockies to secret place... oh... no secret place... not say that. His sockies smell sweaty... can I have them?"

"You can go," Eades said and turned to her as the disheveled-looking man left the room.

Oh, dear, he was not pleased she hadn't told him about Scott. Was she about to be in trouble?

Lola was still looking down at Sassy and the little Frenchie covered her eyes with her paws. Lola knew exactly how she felt.

"Did you really think you could hide that from me?" Eades snapped.

"I didn't hide it from you." Lola knew that she was probably back on his suspect list. That didn't bother her, she had a good alibi but if he shut her out of the case it was different. She needed to prove Scott's innocence. If he was arrested, he could lose his business and his reputation.

"You have military experience!" This wasn't a question but a statement and she nodded.

"If what you said about stopping the knife attack was true, then you had the skills to kill Carmine." Eades's eyes were boring into her but Lola didn't flinch. She had faced down worse than this.

"Why would I kill her?"

"Motives are funny things. Some people just like to kill."

Lola felt the blood run from her face. She knew that the statement was factually correct but it insulted her to her very core.

Eades sighed. "I don't think it was you, I just had to ask the question and your reaction said all I need to know. However, is there anything else I NEED to know?"

"Linc, Martin Hall, is also military trained, he has the skills to do this, but he has no connection to the victim." Lola hated doing this but she had to, if she kept it quiet it would make Linc look even more guilty.

"Who is he here with?" Eades asked.

"He's on his own." Lola hated saying the words.

"That's mighty suspicious. From what I've seen, there are no other single male guests. Was he on the prowl?"

"Well, he's been chatting me up all day."

"Linc, nice," Sassy said and she tapped her paw on Eades's leg.

He gave her a funny look and Sassy said it again. "Why is she grumbling at me like that?"

"Maybe she thinks Linc is a good guy?"

The look Eades gave Lola was enough to shut her up, why had she even said that? All she had done was make Eades even more suspicious.

SEPARATION

"We need to check Matt's alibi," Eades said and he shouted for Wilson.

The PC scrambled into the room.

"Find me, Marilee... Smith."

"Sir." Wilson was gone and there was an uncomfortable silence in the room.

"I appreciate you letting me help out on this," Lola said. "I want you to know that I am not involved with Linc, we only met today. I'm not in the habit of forming short-term relationships. I will help you as much as I can." It was as if the words just kept spewing out of her and she eventually stopped them.

Eades sat back in his chair and tipped the front legs off the floor. "You're here because you have knowledge of the victim, don't think that we are partners." He let the chair fall back to the floor, creating quite a bang.

Lola didn't flinch but Sassy did. She let out a scream and Eades jumped a little. Lola reached down pretending to calm the Frenchie. "Shush, Sassy, it's all right," she said as she hid a chuckle.

The door opened and PC Wilson held it while Marilee walked in. The woman had long straight blonde hair and was beautiful. It was hard to guess her age but Lola thought she must be pushing her forties maybe even in her fifties. Slim, her build was athletic and she was wearing a lot of makeup. It didn't hide a look of fatigue that hung on her like a cloak.

"Take a seat, we just want to ask you a few questions. I'm Detective Sergeant Eades and this is my associate, Lola Ramsay."

Lola was curious that just after they had words, that he introduced her as his associate. Was this to relax her or put pressure on the witness?

"It's true then," Marilee said.

There was sadness on her features but it was not raw. It was more the sadness you had when a distant person passed and if Lola's information was right she had worked closely with Carmine for many years. Did that mean anything?

"What's true?" Eades asked.

Marilee looked at Lola and then him, her eyebrows drew in as she tried to work out if he was teasing her. "That Carmine is dead."

"Yes, it's true," Eades opened his notebook, "what do you know about it?"

"Just that a body had been found and that it was believed to be Carmine. Some are saying she had a heart attack, others that it was murder."

"What was your relationship with Carmine?" Eades asked.

For a moment Marilee looked phased. Lola thought it was more information overload than guilt. She had expected Eades to give her more details and when he didn't her mind tried to fill in the gaps and overloaded itself.

"I... I sang on her records and performed live when she toured."

"How did you like that?" Eades asked.

"She sad but also happy and feeling guilty about it all," Sassy said as she made her way over to Marilee.

"Oh, my, look at you." Marilee scooped Sassy onto her knee and placed kisses on her head. "Sorry, what was that?"

"I asked how you felt about working for Carmine? Did you enjoy it? Was she easy to work for?" Eades had his pen poised over his notebook.

Marilee sighed. "I loved it at first. We were famous, it was glamorous, and we were making money, not much but for a young lass. I was young and single and thought it was what I wanted."

"But now?" Lola asked as sympathetically as she could.

"I've hated it for years. I'm still single because there was never time to court. I hurt my back, the money is all but gone so I'm living on the breadline, and Carmine is a... well, let's just say she's not the easiest to work with."

"Why didn't you quit?" Lola asked.

"We signed contracts years ago. At the time all we wanted was the excitement, we would have sold our souls... guess what... we did."

"Where were you between 12 and 2 pm?" Eades asked.

Marilee looked as if she was trying to remember but there was something a little exaggerated about it. She was hiding something, Lola was sure of it.

"Oh, I was with Becki and Sue between 10 and 11.30. We all met with Carmine at this stone circle for a bite to eat at 11.30 and I left there with Matt Wallens around 12.30." She closed her eyes, was that a sign that she was lying? "He was hoping to find a way out of my contract for me."

"Looks like you found one!" Eades said.

"This is not the way I wanted it to end," Marilee said and a tear slid down her cheek.

It was a genuine tear, but Lola was not sure what it was for. The death of Carmine, the death of Marilee's own dreams, guilt, something was wrong with the woman's testimony but she couldn't say what.

"I think that's all we need," Eades said, "you may go."

Lola wanted to say something but she couldn't think what and after all, Sassy was comforting the woman, she wouldn't do that if Marilee was the killer... would she?

"Who do you think could have done this?" Lola asked.

There was a flicker of something in Marilee's eyes. She thought she knew, then it cleared. "I saw the spa manager have a real fight with her. He was fuming about how she was damaging the reputation of the place. Maybe he lost his temper."

"She hiding something," Sassy said but she reached up and kissed Marilee's cheek.

"Thank you, you can go," Eades said.

Marilee kissed Sassy and put her down. "If I can help at all I will. I no longer liked Carmine, but I cared for her... if that makes sense."

Once she was gone Eades stood. "I need to visit the gents' and have a walk. We will talk to this manager and others. I will get Wilson to sort that for us in about 15 minutes. Go have a stretch."

Lola nodded. She wanted to speak to Alice and to Sassy and she could hardly do that in front of the detective.

She just hoped that he wasn't going to be looking into her or Linc, she just hoped that this wasn't an excuse to separate them while he made his move.

NASTY BUSHES

"Oh, sweet grass, so good to have wee wees." Sassy was squatting on the grass and letting out a sigh of such pleasure that it made Lola chuckle. It had been a long day for the little dog.

"Let's take a walk and then go see our friends," Lola said.

Sassy set off across the wide-open area looking for birds to chase. Lola let her run after the first one and then called her back, scratching her behind her ears when she came. Lola sat down on the grass, and Sassy curled up on her lap.

"Could you tell who took the body to the bushes?" Lola asked.

Sassy tilted her head from side to side, for a moment Lola thought that she had spotted another bird, and then she realized that she was thinking.

"How know?" Sassy turned to look up at Lola and the confusion was deep in her amber eyes. This needed a different approach.

"Could you sniffies another person under the bushes?"

"No."

"Could you sniffies people who had touched Carmine?"

"Lots of people touched her. So many sniffies but couldn't tell there."

Did this mean she couldn't smell over the Patouchi? Or she couldn't tell when they had touched her or if it had been there at the murder scene? "What about the scent of other people in the bushes? Was there one in particular?"

"Nasty bushes not good to sniff. Lots of people sniffies on grass."

"Too strong for you?"

Sassy looked confused. "Not good in nossies, make poorly, so I not sniffies."

That comment reminded Lola that she had heard that rhododendrons were highly poisonous to dogs. That even the leaves were poisonous. Did that make the scent bad? Was that why Sassy couldn't tell her who had been there?

Lola remembered Alice telling her that even the honey from rhododendron was poisonous. There was a case of Greek soldiers being poisoned by contaminated honey as far back as the 4th century. In more recent times, honey poisoning had happened in Turkey. Such rhododendron poisoning was called honey intoxication or mad honey disease. The symptoms were weakness, dizziness, nausea, vomiting, and even death was possible at higher doses.

"What you thinking?" Sassy pawed at Lola's hand to encourage her to stroke her again.

"Who's sniffies were on the grass near the body?" Lola asked.

"Greasy man, grumpy man, Hart, lady we just saw and lots of other people. Really good sniffies, someone had chicken and cake." Sassy was looking up at Lola, all eager and happy. "We could have cake."

"Let's go see what we can find."

Sassy spun in a circle and set off back to the building. She would be searching for Tilly and Alice, both of whom spoiled her constantly. Lola wondered if they could help her out as Carmine had so many enemies. Maybe, her friends could get some clues for her.

* * *

Lola and Sassy crossed the rooftop to find Alice, Tilly, Tanya, Louisa, and Sam still sitting at the same table. They seemed relaxed and the table was covered with various food and drink items.

"How's it going?" Tilly asked.

"There are a lot of suspects."

Sassy was begging in front of Alice, who was handing down little bits of cake.

"Where's Linc?" Lola looked around but couldn't see him. Was she a little disappointed that he wasn't waiting for her? Had he gone to find another woman?

"He was trying to find out who was where when this happened, he keeps bringing back the information." Tilly said. "I've been speaking to a few people as well."

"That's what I like to hear, what have you found out?"

Tilly leaned forward and wrinkling her small nose, she pushed back her round glasses and cleared her throat. "Lots, the three backing singers were all together and can give each other alibis. Carmine was stalking Bruce and he was getting fed up with it. He's also auditioning for a role in a new movie but... Hart is also auditioning."

"That's interesting," Lola said as she felt Sassy slump down on her feet. It looked like Alice had stopped spoiling her.

"That's what I thought, it's a very lucrative role, some movie bringing back aging action characters. Now, if Carmine was to create a stink about either of them it would cost them the part."

"That's a pretty good motive."

"Exactly." Tilly shook her head. "No one needs proof nowadays, spread some gossip and careers, lives are ruined."

"Really, Tilly!" Louisa said. "You agree with what these men have got away with over the years?"

"No, not at all. I believe in justice, but, I also believe in innocent until proven guilty."

Lola agreed with both of them, at times the modern world was hard to negotiate. Things had to change, but she knew that innocent people did have their lives destroyed; after all, she was doing this because she believed Scott was innocent.

"Can you find out for me if any of our suspects had a reason to be in the stone circle today?" Lola asked.

"Oh, that one's easy." Tilly chuckled and pushed back her glasses. "I spoke to Jeffery Hyde-Whyte, there was a meeting there with Carmine, the singers, the two managers, and Hart. He didn't know what it was about but they wanted food and drinks taken out there and then privacy."

That corroborated what she had already found out. It meant they all knew about the area and had all been in the area. Did it make one of them the killer? It was likely, but how had Carmine been left there. "Do you know what time?"

"It was for a brunch, early lunch so I think it finished about midday, maybe starting around 11.30. Jeffery said they were not there long."

"That's really good, can you find out if anyone had patchouli?" Lola asked.

Tilly's eyes narrowed. "How would I do that?"

"Sorry, it's just that Carmine smelt of it and it is quite rare. Maybe it is used in the treatment rooms for massage or something?"

"I will ask Susan, she is one of the waitresses and she has been really helpful."

"Thanks, knock on the door and let me know if you find out anything."

Lola felt as if she had even more suspects, but how could she narrow it down and who was the last one to leave this meeting? Was it Fred? The man's temper could certainly make him a killer and he had a motive.

Lola checked her watch and knew she had to get back to Eades. Though she had lots of new information, none of it led anywhere. As she walked across the conservatory she saw Marilee. The singer was holding her head and leaning back on a sofa. Two other blonde women were talking to her with their backs to Lola.

"Why did they talk to you alone?" one of them said. "After all, we were all together."

"These ladies on grass," Sassy said.

"I wonder if Hart will get his ring back?" the other said.

"Just drop it, will you." Marilee closed her eyes.

Lola felt a jolt of energy. The ring, was the ring missing? If so, that was it, that was her way to solve the murder.

THE RING

When Lola made her way back to the office Wilson was showing Eades a report. She recognized it as the preliminary report on the body. They would not have everything yet, but it was a start.

"This is interesting reading," Eades said and his eyes bored into Lola.

Oh, dear, he knew about the patchouli and she was a suspect again. "In what way?"

"The scent on the body was patchouli, used in the Middle East to hide the scent of death, you and anyone else who had been stationed out there would know that. You didn't tell me."

"We're at a spa, she had treatments and perfume, I didn't think what she smelt like was relevant."

"Hmmm." Eades turned back to Wilson. "Send the manager in and then check all the guests, staff, etc. for military experience."

"Before you do," Lola turned to Eades, "was there any jewelry on the body?"

Eades scanned the report. "Diamond stud earrings and a couple of rings."

"The rings, was one a large diamond, and I mean large, on a gold chain around her neck?"

Eades read again. "No, why!?"

"She was wearing a very large ring around her neck on a chain when I first saw her and Hart asked for it back. Well, I think it was the ring that he was asking for as she clutched onto it when he asked."

Eades looked at the report again and his eyebrows narrowed. "There was evidence of trauma where something had been ripped off of her." He thought for a moment. "Check that with Jinny. If needs be, get her to view the body and the property."

Wilson froze on the spot, his face white, his eyes wide.

Sassy chuckled. "He nearly pooped."

"Go man, she won't bite you." Eades shook his head as Wilson left the room. "He's a good lad but women terrify him."

Eades took another look at the report. "We have a time of death, it was between 12.30 and 1.30, where were you?"

"I would be with my friends, you can check with them if you need to. However, I think we found the knife at 1.30 and no one was in the area." Was Linc in the area? He could have been. He was there when she went back later and he could easily have been hiding.

He smiled. "Nah, I know it's not you but you need to be open with me."

There was a knock on the door and PC Harris showed in a distinguished-looking gentleman in the Spa's uniform. It was a little like a tuxedo and made him look like a butler. The man was in his early fifties, his back was ramrod straight, his nose raised above the stench below – well, that was the impression he gave Lola. Pale skin covered a pinched face and narrow lips. The man carried an air of superiority that made Lola wonder if he was an aristocrat.

"This is the spa manager, Jeffery Hyde-Whyte," Harris said. "Do you need anything else, sir? If not I will rescue, PC Wilson."

"No, you go." Eades turned to Jeffery who was standing with his hands in the small of his back, his nose still high in the air. "Sit," Eades barked.

Jeffery pulled a face as if the sound was distasteful to him and moved with great care to take a seat. "Why am I here? I have a spa to run and you people have already caused immeasurable damage to its reputation."

"Us people!" Eades looked at Lola and widened his eyes. "Us people have caused the damage and not the murder of one of your guests." He turned back and let his eyes burn into the manager.

"Well, well, of course, but one of ours would not have done this. You should be investigating that and not harassing my guests."

Sassy was sniffing at his legs and Jeffrey pushed her away and dusted down his trousers.

"I heard you had a falling out with Carmine. Tell us what happened." Eades said.

Jeffery's lips went even thinner but then he let out a sigh and seemed to slump in his chair. "I was just so tired of her histrionics. The phone, the shouting, the demands for the purest water, run over stones from the Himalayas. I had more complaints this morning than all my years here put together. I have given out 15... yes, 15 free vouchers because people's visits have been ruined. We pride ourselves on relaxation and our de-stressing environment. Clinton Hall is the perfect place to go to unwind."

"So you wanted to be rid of her," Lola said.

"Yes..." His mouth widened into a great big O. "No, no, not in the least. I didn't kill her. I wouldn't, I'm vegan."

Eades chuckled. "Maybe she ate meat!"

"No, no, I love all life I wouldn't hurt anything, ask the staff, I won't even kill spiders."

"Smellies sharp," Sassy said.

"What?" Lola asked.

"I wouldn't hurt a fly," Jeffery said and his lip was wobbling. He bit it to try and stop the movement and a tear ran down his face.

"He hiding something and he... like a lemon," Sassy said.

Lola thought about that one and the only thing she could come up with was bitter.

"Why are you so bitter?" Lola asked.

"I hate my guests to be disturbed. Clinton Hall should be an oasis of calm, joy, and relaxation. She was disturbing that and I was angry. My guests mean the world to me."

Eades was skipping through his notebook. "Ahhh," he said, "Your guests..." Eades tutted. "Not for much longer if the owners have their way."

"What?!" Jeffery's face was even whiter and for a moment it turned into a snarl.

"I heard that they are trying to replace you with a cheaper version." Eades was smirking in a most unpleasant way and it worked. Lola could almost see steam coming out of the manager's ears.

"They are always cost-cutting. This house is a great piece of British heritage, it deserves to have a manager who cares for it and one who can add the needed touch of class." Jeffery folded his arms across his chest as if that was the end of it.

"Really," Lola said. "It's had a somewhat chequered history. Used as a maggot factory, I believe!"

The man's face was so red it looked like he might blow a gasket. "That was just a short period of time. It is a beautiful building that deserves our respect. Now, is there anything else I can help you with?" He stood.

"Sit," Eades shouted this time.

Sassy pulled back from her sniffing and into a sit. "Sitting," she said. "I good dog."

Lola reached down and stroked her.

"I see." Eades made notes in his book. "So, if Carmine or lots of guests complained to the owners... it might be the excuse they needed to get rid of you."

Jeffery's face was like a cartoon showing the extreme of all emotions but then it calmed and there was a look of victory in his eyes. "Yes, but not as much of an excuse as if there was a murder on my watch." Folding his arms he looked very superior for just a second and then his face crumpled. "I'm going to be fired, aren't I!"

"I couldn't possibly say." Eades's face wore a look of delight. "When was the last time you saw her?"

"I and 2 of the girls delivered a meal out to the stone circle. Ms. Rivers and a group of people were there for a meeting. It was arranged by Matt Wallens and attended by Ms. Carmine, Mr. Wallens, Mr. Stilby, Mr. Bowers and the three blonde women who I believe are singers. I will have their names on the records but I don't know them off hand."

"What time was that?" Eades asked.

"Around 11.30."

"Did you see her afterward?"

"No, I didn't go back out to clear up, I believe that was Susan Miller. I could ask her."

Lola could tell by the lack of spark in Eades's eyes that he didn't think Jeffery had done this. Lola agreed with him. Though it was possible that he had gotten angry and struck out it seemed unlikely. However, it had to be one of the people at that meeting, didn't it? Why was Jinny not there, did that make her a suspect?

THE LAST WITNESS

When Jeffery left the room, PC Harris popped her head around the door. "Sir, it seems that no necklace or large diamond ring was found on the body. Jinny did confirm that Ms. Rivers always wore it." Harris rolled her eyes.

Lola wondered how difficult it had been to get that information and if Jinny was still as distraught.

"It was an engagement ring from Hart Bowers, very expensive and the two of them had fought over it on numerous occasions."

"You say expensive, what sort of money are we talking about?" Eades asked.

Harris gulped. "It's a 7-carat ring and was bought for over £1 million; apparently, it's worth even more now and she was always threatening to sell it but didn't. Jinny said she never took it off unless she was swimming."

"Phew!" Eades let out a whistle. "We need to find that ring. That is one powerful motive. You said it was from her engagement to Hart?"

Harris nodded.

Eades turned to Lola. "I think we have a winner. He asked for it back, you heard that?"

"I did." Lola reached down and picked up Sassy. While Eades looked at his notes and asked Harris another couple of questions she whispered into the little bull-dog's ear. "When you see people can you sniffies for a diamond and let me know if they have a big one on them."

Sassy nodded. This had been a game they played at a recent party. Lola had taught Sassy to sniff out a diamond and had hidden one and delighted the crowd by getting her to find it. It all came about because Alice had told her about diamond ore sniffing dogs from the past. Lola couldn't resist trying it out and Sassy had been amazing. It appeared that dogs could smell the carbon that leached out of the diamond, but who knows, for Sassy could rarely explain what scents were like, in a way that a human could understand.

"If you find it you get a sausage," Lola said.

"I find it." Sassy jumped onto the floor. "Let me out, I go searches!"

"Hold your horses, little pooch." Lola chuckled and Sassy sat on the floor and stared at the door.

"Does she need to go?" Eades asked.

Lola wondered if she should tell him that the dog could sniff out diamonds, but she decided not to. "No, she's fine."

"Send Hart in," Eades said.

Harris did just that.

Hart took a seat and smiled at them.

"He sad," Sassy said. "Proper sad not pretend. No diamond though." Once she had said this Sassy came back to Lola and curled up to sleep.

"You are a violent man, Mr. Bowers," Eades said.

Hart looked at Lola. "No... no, I'm not..."

"There are many witnesses to the attack you made on Scott Brussard."

"Him, I attacked him!" Hart waited for Eades to say something. When Eades stayed quiet, Hart began talking again, suspects often couldn't bear the silence. "I care... cared for Carmine... despite everything that happened. In my mind, marriage is a lifetime commitment, and that... that boy she is with... he was disrespectful. I was simply defending my wife's reputation."

"Ex-wife and you fought with her too." Eades raised his eyebrows and gave Hart his meanest stare.

Hart shifted in his seat but that was all. "She was difficult, one day she wants to divorce me, the next to ruin my reputation, the next to get back together... it was exhausting but I would have given it another go if I thought she was genuine."

"It would have been easy to lose your temper, to strike out, say over a million-pound engagement ring. I would understand that." Eades said. "What made her like that?"

"Some say she was bi-polar... I don't think so... I think she lacked confidence and was just angry that she had wasted her life. Everything came too easily in the early days, and when the world changed, she didn't. If she had moved with the times she would still be a star but she wanted the world to move with her and when she realized it wouldn't it was too late."

"We hear she gave you back the engagement ring," Eades said.

"No." Hart chuckled. "I only ever asked for it to tease her. I knew she would never give it back, but sometimes... I guess I hoped that thinking about it would remind her of happier times."

"Now that she's gone, do you inherit everything?" Eades asked.

Hart chuckled. "I don't know if she has a will. We're technically still married, so if not, I guess so, but... the ring was all there was and I imagine her debts would wipe that out."

"I thought she had properties." Lola had listened to some of Alice's talk earlier and was sure that there was a big house and land somewhere.

"There is the house I bought, but I believe she has remortgaged it." Hart shrugged. "I would still like the ring, I don't mind paying into her estate the value... once it's no longer evidence, of course."

"Why?" Eades asked.

Hart rubbed a hand through his hair. "As I said, we were still married and I would like to remember the good times."

"Your financial situation, how is that?" Eades asked.

"I don't need to worry about money. I took care of what I earned and invested well."

"What about Bruce Powell, you and he are vying for the same movie?" Eades was writing something again, probably to check Hart's financials.

"Ahh, I don't think that Bruce has been so lucky. He likes the bright lights and is always putting on a show. That costs a lot of money. Me, I'm happy at home with my horses. As to the movie, we are not rivals, we could both get a part. I'm still not sure if I want to do it. It would be a long time away from home and I feel as if I'm happier as I am."

"So why did you come here today?" Lola asked.

"He not like that question," Sassy said.

Lola noted that. His body must have had an instant reaction to the question for the dog to pick up on it so quickly.

Hart closed his eyes and then pulled his phone out of his pocket. He scrolled to a screen and then passed it to Lola. She leaned over so that Eades could read it too.

The text read:

I will ruin you.

I will tell the papers you beat me.

I have proof.

Divorce me now or I release it.

I will be at Clinton Hall tomorrow, meet me there.

"That is one good motive for murder," Eades said as he forwarded the text stream to his own phone and then put the phone on the desk. "We'll be keeping this for evidence."

"I understand, but I didn't kill her."

"Why were you angry when you first came in, was it because of this text?" Lola asked.

"That, and because she wouldn't take my call. I wanted to meet outside in private. I kept calling and calling and she just ignored it. I came all this way here and she couldn't pick up the phone."

"That must have made you pretty angry?" Eades pressed.

"Of course, but I wouldn't kill her, I would be more likely to leave."

"You met with a few people around the stones and with Carmine. That is the last time she was seen alive. What happened?"

"Matt was trying to crawl his way back into her good graces. Fred was trying to get her to go on The Escape reality TV show. Marilee Smith wanted out of her contract, Sue Davies wanted more money and a bigger role in the shows, and Becki Webster didn't really care either way."

"And what did you want?" Eades asked.

"I just wanted to be left alone or to have my marriage back. I didn't mind either but I didn't want to be dragged into a gutter war. Carmine could do that sometimes."

"Who was the last person to leave the meeting?" Eades asked.

"I was. I stayed behind to ask her once more to let it go. I invited her for dinner on Wednesday, saying that we could talk."

"What happened?" Lola asked.

"She laughed at me and walked off."

"Did you see her go back to the spa?" Eades asked.

"No, she went in the other direction, behind some big bushes."

"It looks like you were the last one to see her," Eades said. "Did you kill her?"

"No, no, I didn't."

"We'll see." Eades closed his book. "That's all the questions for now, but I will get an officer to process your clothing and all your belongings. Harris!"

"He telling the truth," Sassy said.

"Is that necessary?"

"Now he nervous, but little nervous."

"PC Harris, see that Mr. Bowers is searched, we are looking for a gold chain and a diamond ring, check his locker and any belongings too. Check his clothing for blood and DNA."

"He not got diamond," Sassy said.

Lola believed her, but who had and where were they hiding it?"

ROCK AND A HART

"Who next?" Lola asked as Eades checked his notes.

"I like him for it," Eades said indicating the door that Hart had just walked out of. "I'm expecting them to find that rock on him anytime soon. I hope for Harris's sake that he's not hidden it too well. I'm not sure we've got enough evidence to ask him to bend over."

"Charming," Lola said. "I don't think it's him."

"Why?

She could hardly say that Sassy hadn't smelt the diamond on him but even without that he seemed like a decent man. It would have been sensible for him to walk away, she believed him when he said that he was financially well off enough to not need Carmine and yet he had defended her. That was real emotion, either he still cared for her or he would do it for any woman. Either way, he was a decent man.

"I guess it's just my gut instinct," Lola said.

"He was the last one to leave the scene of the crime before she died. He's her heir, she riled him up earlier, how much more evidence do you need?"

Lola chuckled. "It wasn't him."

"Care to make a wager on that?" Eades said.

"I don't know about that."

"Nothing too much, say the loser has to fetch the winner coffee and cake?"

Lola chuckled. "Are you hungry, we could take a break?"

"Yeah, guess I am. I came here off an all-night shift and I haven't eaten yet. I'll get some refreshments, we can keep interviewing people while we eat. Harris!"

PC Harris fetched them toasted sandwiches, or as Lola would know it grilled cheese and coffee and cake. The food was good and they munched and talked over the case while the next person was found.

"This is Sue Davies," Harris said as she showed a glamorous blonde into the room. She was wearing the normal spa robe but beneath it, she had on a low-cut red bikini and her ample bosom was only just safely inside it.

"How are you doing on checking everyone for military service or links to the Middle East?" Eades asked.

Harris's eyes flicked to Lola and then back to Eades. "I'm still checking, sir. Miss Ramsay here has both and Martin Hall has too, but I'm only halfway through the list and I might have something on Hall, I will let you know soon."

Lola wondered what she had on Linc, and hoped that he was not the killer. If he was he had duped her and she was starting to like him. Could her and Sassy's instincts be that far off?

"Okay, good, bring it to me when you have checked everyone. Double check on Hart Bowers."

"Sir."

Eades turned his eyes to Sue. The woman was in her early fifties but very glamorous. Long blonde hair, sculptured cheek bones on her tanned skin, and big almost swollen red lips. Lola imagined that she had had work done on those. She was patting her eyes and there was some sign that she had been crying.

"You must be so upset, losing a friend like Carmine," Lola said.

Sue almost jerked at the question, as if surprised by some part of it.

"Of course, it is so tragic. We could have done so much and it is all such a terrible, terrible waste now." Sue patted her eyes.

Sassy was sniffing at the woman's legs and Lola waited for her little dog to offer comfort, she didn't, but instead, wandered back over and sat next to Lola.

"Not sad, tears for self," Sassy said. "No diamond."

"When did you leave the meeting at the stones?" Eades asked.

"I and the other two singers all left first. Matt and Fred were arguing with Carmine and Hart just looked sad."

"You were there to get out of your contract too, were you?" Lola asked.

This time the shock on her face was easy to spot. "No, I wanted to renegotiate, of course, who doesn't, but I love the life we had. I wanted to do more. I wanted Carmine to go on The Escape, I was even hoping to go on as well. If we all did it, it would have been great but the other two... well, they are so lazy." As she finished she let her robe fall open and crossed her long legs.

Eades shook his head and Lola almost chuckled. This one thought she was a femme fatal.

"Who was lazy?" Lola asked.

"The other two backing singers, Marilee and Becki." She shook her head and folded her arms across her chest boosting her bosom a little and flashing her long eyelashes. There was a touch of disappointment when Eades took no notice.

There was something about Sue that was a little unpleasant. She seemed to be the sort of person who would blame everyone but herself for everything. "If only they would have put in some effort then maybe we would still be on top. We were good, are good but there was so much bickering that... well, it drifted away."

"Do you have an alibi for the murder?" Eades asked. He didn't give a time and Lola knew that this was deliberate. He wanted to see where she had been all day.

"We are each other's alibi, we were together all day." She snorted out a laugh. "It will probably be the last time, but maybe the press coverage will give me a spotlight." A smile crossed her face. "Yes, this could be the start of something good." She arched her back and pushed out her chest even more. "I still have what it takes and my voice is as good as ever. Maybe I could even cover Carmine's songs. Oh, this is exciting."

Lola let her mouth drop open. Carmine was not even cold and the woman was planning her career move, that was cold.

"Do you need me for anything else? I ought to strike while the iron is hot and see if I can get a deal."

Eades shook his head. "You can go for now, but you have just given yourself a motive."

"Talent is no motive," Sue said. "It just is. Oh, I must check my contract too, if Carmine's songs hit the charts I could be in for a nice payout."

That was a thought. Would there be any income in Carmine's songs? When Elvis died it had been huge... but Carmine, would it be enough to give someone a motive?

A SUSPICIOUS LINC

When Sue left the room, Harris popped her head around the door.

"Come in," Eades said.

Harris shut the door behind her and glanced at Lola, why was she nervous?

"Spit it out, woman," Eades said and waved at the chair.

Harris sat down and opened her notebook. "The only people I can find with military experience are Miss Ramsay and Martin Hall. Both served in the same region around the same time."

"Leave Miss Ramsay for now." Eades waved at her to continue.

"Mr. Hall infiltrated ISIS and had a lot of knowledge of the local area. He worked undercover for several years and contact was lost at one point. Though it is unconfirmed, I believe he was in the SAS. He has received multiple commendations including a Victoria Cross for bravery."

Lola felt a touch of pride but she could see that Harris was nervous about something. Losing contact was not unusual in such a situation, it could be a red flag, some people went native, but it could also simply be a factor of safety. When you were deep undercover reporting in could get you killed, you tended to do so as little as was needed.

"However," Harris glanced at Lola, "he left the army under dubious circumstances." Harris checked her notes again as if she might find something new there.

"Dubious?" Eades said.

"No one will say why, his time wasn't up, it wasn't medical, though he has been injured, and there seems to be bad blood. Of course, much of what he did is classified but I get the feeling that he was thrown out."

"We can't work on feelings," Eades said. "Was he dishonorably discharged or not?"

"No, but his ex-commanding officer does not like him. He said, and I quote, 'that man left at the time as a lot of money went missing, and at the same time, a whole village was wiped out'." Harris wiped her forehead and then checked her notes again. "No one could prove who did it. No one will say it was Hall, some stick up for him, but..."

"Well now, it looks like your Linc has a bit of a chequered past."

Lola felt her heart falter. Was Linc the sort of man who could do that? Her stomach turned at the thought of it. Wiping out a village for money, was that the man she had started to like? Was that the man that Sassy liked?

"Let's not jump to conclusions," Lola said even though she knew it was hard to do anything else."

"Go get him," Eades said and turned to Lola. "It doesn't look good. The man has the skills to be a gun for hire and he has the opportunity. I will need to run his financials."

"You don't have enough for a warrant." Lola felt defensive and knew that it was not the right play.

"Then I'll ask permission." Eades smiled, he knew that a person's reaction to such a request could tell you a lot.

Harris knocked and let Linc into the room. He stood stiffly as if he was back in the military and something about it set Lola's nerves on edge.

Sassy, however, went over to him and sat in front of him. Her little tail was wagging as she stared up at the man with a look of sheer adoration. "Good man," she said.

Lola was torn, she wanted to trust Linc, she wanted to trust Sassy, but she had to follow the evidence.

"Sit, Mr. Hall." Eades pointed at the chair. "We want to ask you a few questions about your past." Eades reached below the desk, Lola could see him opening a small brown bottle and putting it against a handkerchief.

Taking the handkerchief he passed it to Linc. "What does that smell of?"

Linc took a sniff and handed it back. "It is patchouli."

"Where have you come across it before?"

"Afghanistan, when I was undercover. What is the relevance of this?"

Lola was watching him closely and either he was a really good actor or he didn't know that Carmine had been covered in the herb.

"It was used to hide the scent of the body," Eades said.

Lola noticed a slight tension in Linc's jaw. It didn't look like hiding a lie, maybe just worry about the significance of this information.

"What do you have to say about that?" Eades asked.

"Are you sure?" Link looked cool and calm, if he was guilty he was good at hiding it.

"We will have it analyzed," Eades said, "but the scent is pretty easily recognizable."

"No, what I meant is, are you sure that is why it was at the scene?"

Lola let out a breath. They had immediately jumped to the conclusion that the oil had been used for some nefarious purpose, maybe it was just there?

"Why else would it be there?" Eades shook his head and folded his arms leaning back as if the matter was closed.

"We're at a health spa, there are other uses for it." Linc looked at Lola and there was a touch of disappointment in his eyes. "I've heard it is good for anxiety and mood and can also be used for pain relief."

"So, you're quite the herbalist now, are you?" Eades was not believing any of this.

"When you live with tribal people you learn the remedies they use and this particular oil had many uses."

"Maybe, I should check your finances?" Eades said.

"Go ahead, I give you my permission... as I'm sure you can't get a warrant." Linc kept his eyes on Eades and didn't flinch.

"That is very good of you. Where were you between 12 and 2 pm?"

Linc turned to Lola. "As you probably already know, for some of that time I was walking the grounds, alone."

"So you have no alibi!" Eades was smiling at that.

"That's right."

"Now, we need to look into your past, why did you leave the army?"

Linc stiffened, he had not expected that question and it was clear he didn't want to answer it.

Lola felt her heart tumble, had she trusted the wrong man?

A BROKEN LINC

"I don't see how my past is relevant," Linc said, his voice was stiff and clipped, he was not happy.

Sassy was still sitting in front of him and staring up with admiring eyes. Normally, she would have been sniffing and looking for clues, including sniffing for the diamond. However, it looked as if Sassy didn't think that Linc was a suspect.

Lola called her over and picked her up. "Sniffy for diamond," she whispered in Sassy's ear. "Is Link bad?" She put Sassy down.

The Frenchie shook herself. "Not bad," she said and then went over to Linc. Lola had to bite back a chuckle as the little dog took in great big sniffs of air, circling around Linc in a most suspicious-looking manner.

Linc, however, was not seeing the Frenchie. His eyes were locked on Eades. They were like two feral dogs, circling each other and watching for a weakness.

"No diamond, good man," Sassy said and she sat leaning against Linc's leg. "He stressed, worried, sweaty like you when wake from bad dreams."

Charming!

That was interesting. The conversation had obviously taken the man back to a memory of the past. Was this guilt that he was feeling or was it something else?

Eades had been waiting Linc out, but eventually, he had to speak. "You see, what I think, is that you massacred that village and took the money. I think you got a taste for it and I think that someone paid you to kill Carmine. Tell me who and it will be better for you."

Link looked at Lola and she felt his eyes asking for her belief. All she could give him was an almost imperceptible nod. The disappointment he felt was well hidden but clear.

"You are asking the wrong people, the wrong questions. It was not me who committed those crimes and I did nothing here." He swallowed and crossed his arms over his chest.

Sassy pawed at his leg and Linc looked down and picked up the Frenchie.

"Good man," Sassy said and Lola believed her.

"You have the skills to do this, you have the opportunity and money could easily be your motive. With your dubious past, you are the perfect suspect." Eades checked through his notes as if he might find the answer there.

"I don't know what to say, I didn't kill her, I didn't know her."

"Ahh!" Eades stopped on a page in his book. "You spoke to Carmine, you were rude to her. Maybe you just lost your temper, maybe this was all a mistake?"

"Really! Charge me or let me go." Linc stood, and waited for Eades to say something, when he didn't, Linc turned and marched out of the room.

"That was mighty suspicious," Eades said.

"I don't think so, let me go talk to him. I don't think he did this."

"I'll give you 30 minutes, we have a couple more people to talk to and then I'm taking Hall and Brussard in for more questioning. We can search their lockers and see if we can find that diamond."

"I have an idea about the diamond." Lola shrugged. "I will tell you later if it works."

At the moment, she was sure that Linc wasn't involved. Sassy had been wrong in the past. She had said another killer was a good man and he was, but he had once made a mistake. Lola believed that the Frenchie was right here. Though she could understand Eades' point of view, she didn't feel as if Linc was the killer. But could she be wrong?

* * *

"Track Linc," Lola said once they were out of the room.

Sassy dropped her nose to the floor and set off down the corridor. Her little tail was brandished like a flag wagging as they went.

Sassy went through the dining room and down the stairs and out into the Zen Garden. There in the corner, in the shade, Linc was sitting on a concrete bench.

"I'm sorry that I had to do that," Lola said as she took the bench opposite him.

He shrugged. "I wanted to leave my past behind."

"I understand... but I could do with knowing enough to be able to pull the attack dog off of you."

For a moment he stayed very still and then he reached down to stroke Sassy, she was leaning against him.

"I'm sworn to keep much of it secret but it was not me who took the money and killed those people. I was the one who brought it out into the open. Some very influential people got caught in the fallout and I got beaten and shot for my trouble. I tried to save the village but by the time I escaped, it was too late. If you want confirmation then I can give you people to speak to."

Lola shook her head, she believed him. "I'm sorry."

He shrugged but she could see that there was a slight shake to his hands. This had taken him back to a memory that was best left in the past. "Unfortunately, my career was over," he said. "I was medically discharged as they believed that the beating I received would make me too broken to trust again."

Lola swallowed. "I'm sorry, I do trust you." Though she said the words she wondered if it was too late."

"You might do, but what about Eades? He will keep coming and I have no proof that I didn't do this."

"I think I might know who did. It's only a theory at the moment but I think I can prove it."

"How?"

"Believe it or not, that little one can sniff out diamonds, she can also sniff out blood. Would you take her to the men's changing rooms and ask her to sniffies for both of them and then come back to the conservatory and let me know what she found?"

"Sniffies?"

"Yeah, I know but it's the word she uses." Lola smacked her own head. Had she just told Linc that the dog used a word? "The word she's trained for."

Linc chuckled. "You are crazy, I like it." He reached down and gave Sassy's ears a scratch. "Okay, Sassy, can we go sniffies for diamonds and blood?"

"Me sniffies good," Sassy said in a series of grumbles and groans, she spun around in a circle and stood waiting for Linc to follow her.

Lola just hoped that her instinct was right, otherwise, Linc and Scott were both in trouble.

ONE MORE SUSPECT

Lola made her way back to the conservatory and nipped over to the rooftop to speak to Tilly. Her friends were all enjoying themselves, chatting in the sun and drinking orange juice but Lola could see that people were starting to get antsy. Eades would not be able to keep them pliable for much longer.

"Have you found the killer yet?" Alice asked as she got to her feet, and then her eyes popped wide open. "Where is Sassy? Is she hurt?" Alice's hands went to her chest and everyone at the table was up.

"No, no, she's fine. I sent her with Linc to check something in the men's changing rooms."

Alice rushed forward and engulfed Lola in a hug. It felt good, even though she was still struggling with such displays of emotion. There was just something about Alice that you couldn't resist.

"Oh, you did scare me," Alice said and sat back down.

"Did you find anything out?" Lola asked Tilly.

"Carmine bought the Patchouli oil from the beauty salon. She had an anxiety and pain relieving massage this morning before we all arrived. She then went for a walk with her two managers. Rumor has it that Matt was not happy."

"When we saw her there was only Fred, wasn't there?"

Tilly cocked her head and pushed her glasses back. "That's right. Susan, my waitress source, was outside having a smoke. Matt had stormed off, and they thought he left, he must have come back. Apparently, Carmine did this and if you let her calm down she would forget all about it.."

"Anything else?"

"Yes, I spoke to a lovely waitress, Karen, who served the group out at the stone ring. She said there was a lot of tension. Matt started pushing the idea of Carmine going on some reality TV show. Carmine told him she had already dismissed such an absurd proposal. Fred got really excited and was desperate to get Carmine to go on the show. He was pushing her again and again and she threatened to sack him. That made Matt laugh, and say again, so Carmine said he was gone too. Then Matt was saying she needed to do something or retire gracefully. She lost it at that. Sue Davies, one of the backing singers was really pushing for the TV show too and suggested they all go on it. The other two were not interested and Marilee got very angry and threatened Carmine with the court if she didn't let her be at home next month. Something about an operation."

"Wow, you have got a lot out of them." This all helped Lola with her theory but there was no proof. It also seemed that everyone had a motive, what about the third backing singer? She was the next person they had to interview, could she lead them to the killer, or could she be the killer?

Lola looked down expecting to see Sassy staring up at her. It felt strange to be without the dog and for a moment she had a touch of anxiety. Not bad place, she told herself. Sassy would be back soon and she could cope until then.

"I haven't found much more out, how about you?" Tilly asked.

"A big diamond has gone missing so I have Sassy looking for it."

"That was so wonderful when you taught her to do that," Tilly said. "She won't let you down."

"Oh, is that the one Carmine wears around her neck?" Alice asked. "I would love to see that; can you imagine a man like Hart down on one knee and opening a box with that huge rock inside? It makes me weak at the knees just thinking about it."

Tilly chuckled. "You should get out more. Who knows, your Hart could be out there waiting."

Alice chuckled and her cheeks pinked beneath her short blonde curls. "Oh, I don't know. I'm happy and who wants to open themselves up to heartbreak?"

Lola understood that point of view.

"Better to have loved and lost," Tilly said and there was a distant look in her eye. That was a story Lola must ask her about sometime.

"Thanks, Tilly. I will catch up with you later, we have one more person to interview."

"Can you share who you think it is?" Alice asked.

"Not just yet." Lola chuckled. "Hopefully, soon."

Lola crossed back to the room where the interviews were taking place. The steps she took were slow as she hoped to see Sassy before she went back into the room. It was not to be though, maybe she was still searching the changing rooms, or maybe Linc was treating her to more sausage.

The door was open and Eades had a coffee in front of him. "There's one for you too," he said. "Did you find anything out about Hall?"

"The trouble on his file, he was the one who tried to stop it. Things got messy and it cost him a beating and his commission."

"I didn't think it was him, but there were red flags. I had to ask those questions."

"I know, it's okay."

A knock on the door pulled their attention. Lola took her seat and had a quick sip of coffee. It was only tepid, but it was still good and she took another one while Harris showed in the third backing singer, Becki Webster.

Becki was very similar in looks to the other two ladies. Long blonde hair, a beautiful face, and big blue eyes. There was something serene about those eyes and though she looked good, unlike Sue, she was not hiding or ashamed of her age. Becki seemed to be the most relaxed of all of the people in Carmine's universe. Surely, that was not the face of a killer?

"Please take a seat, Miss Webster," Eades said.

"Mrs." Becki sat down and smiled. She crossed her legs and leaned back, her posture was open and relaxed which was amazing for anyone after today. Even just the stress of the murder and being segregated into areas on your spa day was enough to skyrocket most people's blood pressure. That meant that either Becki was a great actor, or she was really chilled? Lola felt it could be the latter and she could see from the slump in Eades's shoulders that he thought the same.

"How was your relationship with Carmine Rivers?" Eades asked.

Becki smiled. "Carmine could be difficult, the key to working with her was to just let it go. Some people, you can't change."

"Were you trying to renegotiate your contract?" Eades looked a little lost, her answer was not what he wanted.

"No, not really."

"Did you want more money?" Eades was going to push this.

"No."

"Did you want out of your contract?"

Becki smiled. "That would be nice, but we didn't do many shows now. There were just three more this year and next... I don't think any were booked. I could wait until then to retire."

"What do you do now... what can live up to jetting around the world for a famous singer?"

Becki smiled once more and pulled her phone out of her pocket, she scrolled to a picture of two children. They looked to be around 6 years old, a little girl and a boy. "My twins were a total surprise and came late. They are my life, those and my husband... and trust me, touring Skegness on a clapped out old bus loses its appeal after a few years... not that I have anything against Skegness."

"Where were you between 12 and 1 pm?" Eades asked the question but by the look on his face, even he didn't think the answer mattered.

"I was with Marilee and Sue for all of it, for some of it I was with Matt, Fred & Carmine out at the stone circle at the far side of the property."

"Do you know who had a motive to do this?" Eades asked.

"No, but a lot of people could lose their temper with Carmine. She still believed she was a star. Unfortunately, those days didn't last long. In mind, she should have retired with Hart, she would be much happier."

Eades looked at his notebook and sighed. "We might need to ask more questions later."

"Sorry I can't be any more help."

"It's okay, you can go," Eades said and he closed his notebook.

Once the door had closed he turned to Lola. "I have no choice but to arrest Scott."

"It's not him," Lola said. "Give me 30 minutes and then have everyone involved out here in the conservatory. I might have something."

Eades shook his head and for a moment she thought he was going to refuse.

"You have twenty-five. After that, I'm taking Scott in. What I have is circumstantial but I think it would be enough for a conviction."

"Would you be happy putting the wrong man away?"

Eades shrugged his shoulders. "If the evidence points to him, maybe it's your instincts that are wrong?"

DIGGING UP THE CLUES

Lola stepped out of the room and instantly heard Sassy scream. It was an ear-piercing sound. Everyone in the conservatory turned, thinking that the Frenchie must have been slaughtered, or at the very least that someone had trodden on her paw.

Lola could hear the little dog's excitement. "Found it... missed you... Linc good man."

Sassy pulled the lead out of Linc's fingers and raced across the conservatory. Lola bent her knees and braced herself. Sassy launched into the air and landed in Lola's arms, squirming so much that she almost went through them. The image of a greased pig went through Lola's mind as she clutched onto the excited Frenchie. Pulling Sassy to her face she gave and received kisses.

"What did you find?" Lola whispered.

"Blood from nasty lady. No diamond. Missed you."

Lola hugged her once more and turned to see an embarrassed-looking Linc yomping across to her.

"She just pulled out of my hands, she's very strong." He shrugged.

"Did she find anything?"

"Already told you." Sassy plonked her bottom on the floor and stuck out her back legs. It was her protest sit.

"She was very interested in one locker, I don't know who it belonged to. In fact, I don't know which of the three lockers she was interested in!"

"Highest one. Couldn't reach but sniffies really clear. Told Linc to sniffies, but he useless, like you."

Lola chuckled and then realized that Linc thought she was doing it at him. "Sorry." She pointed at Sassy.

"Yeah, she does make some funny noises. I'm not being funny but that dog... well... I've worked with dogs in the army and they had really long noses... Sassy is great but... she has no nose."

Sassy snorted. "Better than yours."

"She is trained to sniff out certain things and you'd be surprised at how accurate she is. I want to see Jinny. Keep an eye on Eades and if he starts to arrest Scott, remind him he gave me time."

"Will do, do you know who it is? Maybe we could get Eades to open the locker?"

"I have a good idea, but we don't have enough evidence to get the locker opened, just yet. Just make sure everyone stays in here and I will be back shortly.

Lola hoped that she would. She had an idea but it was far from clear, could she prove it?

Lola made the short journey up the stairs to the office where Jinny was. PC Wilson was outside the door reading something on his phone. He didn't hear them and Lola crept up to him and then loudly cleared her throat.

The PC tossed his phone into the air and threw his hands up after it. Guilt pinked his cheeks and he nearly tripped as he reached out to stop the phone from falling.

Sassy jumped up and caught the phone and stood in front of him, holding it and wagging her little body.

"Sorry," Wilson said. "She's been quiet and I was just... well, I was..."

"Don't worry, I'm sure you are fine." Lola took the phone from Sassy and handed it back to him.

He grinned and then wiped the phone before knocking and opening the door for her.

Lola stepped inside to see Jinny sitting behind the desk, her head bowed. She looked up and tried to smile but it didn't quite work.

Sassy raced to her and leaned against her leg.

"I left it too late," Jinny said. "If I had told her I loved her... maybe we could have been happy, maybe this would never have happened."

"Don't think like that. Remember the good times and learn, do things differently going forward."

Jinny managed a better smile this time. "I will. Have you found out who did this?"

"I have an idea. You were all here to renegotiate contracts, is that right?"

"Kind of, it was something that Carmine did often. If I'm honest, she used it as a tool. If things weren't going her way she would sack people, well, the ones who wanted to stay. Those who wanted out, she would hold their contract against them."

"Can I see the contracts?"

For a moment Jinny hesitated, then she shrugged. "Of course." Behind her was a box full of papers. She went through it and pulled out a bundle. "This is mine."

Lola took it but this was not the one she wanted. She scanned it but it was a simple employment contract with some pretty draconian measures on who Jinny could work for if she left. Basically, it was no one!

Lola was hoping that she could dig up some clues, that she could dig up a motive, and if she was right, the person with the most to gain was the one who had killed Carmine.

"Here you go." Jinny handed over three contracts. "These are for the backing singers. They are pretty harsh and I know that Marilee was desperate to get out of hers. Could she have done this?"

"I don't think it was her," Lola said. "How is her back?"

"She is struggling with it. She has a disk that needs operating on. She struggles with the dancing. As part of the routine, she used to lift Sue, she can't do that now."

That confirmed something Lola had thought. Even if Marilee had done it she wouldn't have been able to move the body. No way would she be able to drag it beneath those bushes.

"Did she have an operation booked?"

"Yes, for next month... we got a booking just after she found out the date. The two clashed." Jinny looked a little abashed. Maybe she was starting to see the real Carmine.

Lola got the feeling that that happened to a lot of people, and when they did, finally seeing the real Carmine, they wanted out of the relationship pretty quickly. Was that what had led to murder?

CLOSING IN ON THE KILLER

Lola left Jinny alone in the office and made her way down the stairs to the conservatory. "When we get there you need to go find that diamond," Lola said.

Sassy sat in front of her, her big eyes wide and sad.

"What is it?"

"Found blood, and no sausage! Worked really hard, lots of nasty sniffies in wet room and no socks, no sausage."

"I promise I will get you sausage as soon as I can."

A smile came on Sassy's face and she seemed to nod her head. "Promise?"

"I promise."

Sassy was back on her feet and hopping down the stairs. As they passed the kitchen Lola stopped and pushed open the door. A man wearing a chef's hat was just walking past.

"Excuse me," Lola called.

He turned and glared at her. Lola signaled Sassy to sit and let the door close leaving the Frenchie outside.

"What is it, Miss?"

"I wondered if you had any sausage left from breakfast. I'm working with the police and it would help in the investigation." That wasn't really a lie!

The man shook his head and his eyes widened but then he shrugged. "I can put a few in a plastic bag for you."

"Thank you. Just one will be great, cut into small pieces," Lola said and she heard a snort from the other side of the door.

Sassy would have been happy with more than one!

The chef handed Lola a bag and she tucked it into the pocket of her robe. Now, she hoped that her suspicions were right and that she could prove who the killer was before it was too late for Scott.

They made their way back to the conservatory where PC Harris was waiting at the door. "The Boss is looking for you. People are starting to get uppity and he's going to make an arrest."

"Are the three singers in here?" Lola asked.

"Yes, they stayed out on the rooftop after they had been interviewed."

Lola nodded and made her way to the office where Eades was waiting.

"Do you have something for me?" he snapped.

"Nothing concrete but Sassy can find the diamond."

Eades' shoulders slumped and he slammed his notebook shut. "That's it, I'm arresting Scott."

"He has chocolate in his pocket with coconut," Sassy said and she sat in front of Eades smiling up at him.

"You have a chocolate bar with coconut in your pocket."

He raised his eyebrows and reached for his pocket where he pulled out a half-eaten bar of chocolate. "You must have seen it."

"She indicated chocolate by raising her right paw and coconut by tapping it three times. Sassy, what food can you smell?"

Sassy let out a sigh. "Doing circus tricks now." She raised her right paw and tapped it twice."

Lola blinked.

Sassy tapped the paw a third time.

"Now, I've seen everything. There is no way I'm putting this in my report."

"Google ore sniffing and diamond hunting dogs, you will see that it is a thing. I taught her to find diamonds as a trick for a jubilee party. Let's see if she can find it and if we can get the killer to reveal themselves."

Eades nodded. "I guess I've nothing to lose."

Lola opened the door. "Sassy, go find the diamond."

Sassy let out a squeal of excitement. She loved nothing more than to be hunting for something. Though her favorite thing was squirrels, followed closely by birds, she also liked to find things that were hidden. Lola suspected that it was the thrill of using her nose. Dog's noses are so powerful that they see the world through them. Hiding things for them and letting them find the items gives the dog tremendous pleasure and Sassy was no exception.

Lola often wondered how she managed to always find the items or the person she was hunting. Her nose was much shorter than a German Shepherd's or a bloodhound, however, her sense of smell was keen and well developed.

"What now?" Eades asked.

"Now we wait and see if she can find it."

Sassy stopped in front of a woman and turned to look at Lola.

Lola realized that she hadn't told Sassy to only find a big diamond, of course, what was big to a Frenchie?

"Is that our killer?" Eades had set off before Lola could say anything else. Oh, dear, this could be trouble!

NOT THE ONE

Eades had arrived in front of the woman before Lola did. "Miss, can I ask your name?" He pulled out his warrant card and showed it to her.

The woman was in her mid-60's with a friendly face and smiling eyes. She had short grey curly hair and was talking to another woman who was twenty years her junior and probably her daughter.

"Is there a problem?" the daughter asked.

Lola arrived next to Eades. "Are you wearing any diamonds?" Lola asked.

The woman looked confused and then nodded, she showed her hand. "My engagement ring has a diamond."

"Please, forgive us, we are looking for a different diamond."

"Oh, is that why we are here, has there been a theft?" the woman's voice was getting louder and Lola didn't want to give the game away.

"Please, keep your voices down, this will all be over soon," Eades said and pulled Lola away. "Half these people are going to have diamonds. This is just a joke."

"Give me a few more minutes," Lola said.

Eades grumbled but he stepped behind her.

Lola picked Sassy up. "We want a really big diamond," Lola said and she took a slice of the sausage out of her bag. "Bigger than this."

Sassy's eyes were wide. "That's big. Me sniffies good... me hungry."

Lola gave her the piece of sausage.

"Lots of energy now, me findies good."

Lola put Sassy down and, the little dog set off across the room at high speed. Dogs can scent from the scent on an article or the scent waves in the air. Ground scenting was where they would follow the footsteps on the ground but Sassy had her nose up. She was tasting the air almost. Dogs can also take scent in via either nostril so she would move her head from side to side and then she got the smell of something she wanted.

Lola watched as Sassy set off across the conservatory to another group of women; she knew this was not what they wanted but she had to let Sassy work it out.

She could hear the little Frenchie working. "Sniffies, sniffies good, diamonds, here, here, getting closer. How big?" Sassy arrived at the group of women and went around then stopped in front of one. "Diamond, little sniffies, not right."

Sassy set off again and worked her way around the room. "Sniffies from locker and diamond," Sassy said.

"She has something," Lola said to Eades and slowly they crossed the room. Sassy was working her way around to the corner of the conservatory and stopped in front of a corner table. She sniffed at the man leaning back on the sofa, his eyes were closed until Sassy let out a squeal of delight. Matt was no longer wearing the cream jacket to his suit.

"Biggest diamond. Bloody man... no bad word, didn't mean bad word meant man with blood. Diamond, enough for sausage?"

Matt Wallens had sat up and was staring at Sassy. The look on his face was one of confusion until he saw Lola and Eades heading in his direction. Then he looked for an escape. His eyes drifted to the door but it was still guarded by PC Harris. Matt sat back and smiled but it was clear that he was nervous.

"Have you lost your dog?" he asked as Lola and Eades came over.

"What now?" Eades whispered at Lola.

"Sassy find," Lola said.

"In pocket!" Sassy was waving her front paw at him.

"Oh, no, it's a chocolate bar," Eades said and started to walk away.

Lola noticed that everyone was looking at them and that people were gathering around. "Mr. Wallens, can you confirm where you were at the time of Carmine's death?"

"I already told you this," he said.

Sassy had gone over to him and was pawing at his trouser pocket. Matt tried to push her away.

"It's going to be so embarrassing when she grabs a chocolate bar," Eades said. "Why did I let you do this?"

"You told us you were here before the meeting and that you left the meeting with Marilee."

"That's right," he said but the color dropped from his face as he realized that the three backing singers were all staring at him. Sue and Becki looked from him to Marilee and then to Lola.

"I lied, I'm sorry," Marilee said. "He promised he would get me out of my contract if I said I was with him. I didn't know that she was dead then."

Matt had forgotten Sassy. Slowly, she went up to him and balancing on her butt, she sat up into a beg. Putting her nose forward, she reached into his pocket and pulled out a chain, attached to a huge diamond. Sassy picked it up and ran over to Eades. "Not silly, diamond and chocolate very different sniffies." She was holding the chain with the diamond dragging on the floor beneath her feet.

Eades's mouth was wide open.

"You killed her!" Sue shouted and launched herself at Matt.

Eades managed to grab hold of her robe and she was stopped in midflight. With her arms waving around about her she looked like a giant dove of peace. However, the stream of insults coming from her mouth hardly fit that image.

Eades took the diamond.

Sassy ran to Lola. "Sausage."

Lola handed her a piece down and noticed that her friends and Linc were also watching. The look of pride on their faces warmed her heart.

"I found that," Matt said. "I didn't kill her, why would I?"

MONEY IS ALWAYS A MOTIVE

"You have no evidence," Matt said. "Why would I kill her, she was my only client?"

"I think this rock is enough of a motive, how much is it worth?" Eades held the diamond up.

"I found it, or she gave it to me." Matt ran a hand through his greasy hair and leaned back. He was trying to look cool.

Sue snarled and tried to break free.

"Harris," Eades shouted and the PC came over and took Sue from him. "You just let us handle this," Harris said in a surprisingly soothing voice, and Sue seemed to relax while she led her away.

"But, you do have a motive, don't you?" Lola said.

Matt looked a little nervous but he shook his head. "No."

"I've read your contract."

"Did you have a warrant? You had no right; it won't hold up in court without a warrant." A bead of sweat ran down his forehead and dripped onto his robe. He wiped at his face and pushed his hair out of his eyes.

Lola chuckled. "That might be true if Eades here had done it, but I'm not police, and I asked Jinny if I could see them and she was happy to let me."

"Proves nothing," Matt said.

"It proves that if she fired you, then you would lose all rights to her music after her death."

"But... but..." His face crumpled and he shut up. "I want a lawyer."

"Oh, that is evil," Alice said. "Carmine's records will hit the charts now, once a light like hers has gone out everyone wants to hear her. That will be one huge payday."

"This is all circumstantial," Matt said. "Unless you're going to arrest me, I'm leaving now."

Alice let out a hoot of laughter. "Of course, they're going to arrest you."

Eades stepped forward. "Matt Wallens, I'm arresting you on the suspicion of murdering Carmine Rivers. You do not have to say anything, but it may harm your defense if you do not mention when questioned something that you later rely on in court. Anything you do say will be taken down and may be used in evidence."

"We need to check his locker," Lola whispered to him. "I sent Sassy in there and I think there is blood in it."

Eades pulled Matt to his feet and spun him around, he took handcuffs from his belt beneath his jacket and put them on. "Before we go, we will just visit your locker," Eades said.

Matt's face was now as white as his robe.

Lola, Sassy, Eades, Harris, and Matt made their way to the men's locker room. They had taken Matt's key from his pocket and were looking for the locker.

"This way," Sassy said.

The locker room was lots of different nooks and crannies and the little Frenchie either remembered the way or she could scent her way to the locker.

"Follow her," Lola said.

Eades shrugged. "I will believe anything but I'm not putting it in my report that I followed a dog to a locker. They will lock me up and throw away the key.

Lola chuckled. "Maybe the layout is the same as the ladies?"

"Ahhh, that sounds more likely."

When they turned the corner Sassy was sitting in front of a batch of lockers. "Top one," she said.

"It is number 156," Eades said and shook his head as he realized Sassy was sitting in front of it.

Eades pulled on some gloves and taking the key, he opened the locker and sorted through. The cream jacket was hung there and the sleeve had three round circles of red.

"Blood, I sniffies blood on cloth and shoes."

"Bag those," Eades said.

"It's just ketchup," Matt tried to protest but no one was believing him.

Lola watched as a couple of uniformed officers took Matt away. He was still denying everything but the conviction had gone out of his voice.

"Bag all the items in that locker," Eades said as a crime scene officer began to take items out of it.

"I guess that Scott is free to go?" Lola said.

"Of course." Eades turned to walk away but turned back. "Thank you, Miss Ramsay... and thank you, Sassy. You were both a big help, just don't tell my boss." With a smile, Eades walked out of the room.

THE SCARE IN THE CROW

Within half an hour the spa had returned to its normal operation. People were swimming and relaxing and talking once more. The murder had caused a buzz but everyone seemed able to relax once more and enjoy the rest of the day.

"What should we do now?" Alice asked. "I feel awfully guilty for bringing you here today, and for the terrible circumstances..."

"Don't," Lola said. "It was lucky we were here."

"I want another swim," Tanya said. "That pool is just too glorious to leave."

"I'm up for that." Alice was bouncing up and down on her heels, her orange robe flapping about around her like a fiery dragon.

"I might just go for a walk, I'm sure Sassy would prefer that."

"You should come with us." Sam shrugged his shoulders. "We have some tidying up to do."

Lola smiled and indicated for them to lead on. As they walked across the grass to the corner opposite the stones, Sam threw the ball for Sassy. Despite the busy day, the little Frenchie raced across the grass, still full of energy.

"We're sorry for this," Sam said. His shoulders were down and he seemed worried.

"Don't be," Lola said. "If there hadn't been a murder, it would have been a lot of fun."

"I sniffies chicken," Sassy said and raced off to the corner where a remote copse of trees stood all alone.

Lola could see a flash of white in the undergrowth and a smile crossed her face. It was lovely that Sam and Louisa had done this.

As they entered the trees Lola did a double take and felt a touch of adrenaline spike in her stomach. Over to the side was another body. The look on her face must have said it all for Sam and Louisa chuckled.

"I said it looked good," Louisa said.

"It really does, what is it?" Lola asked.

Sassy was sniffing what looked like a body as they approached.

"Sniffies of chicken, but no chicken here." Sassy sat down and looked up at Lola with an adoring smile. "Any sausage left?"

Lola handed a bit down.

"That is so realistic." Lola leaned forward and touched the body which turned out to be a bundle of cardboard packed into a robe with a piece of wood in some tights as a leg and a hat over a wig.

"We smeared it with chicken, hoping that Sassy would lead you to it."

"She did. This is amazing." Lola couldn't tell them that Sassy had already told her it was chicken and that there was none there. Without the dog's input, she would have thought this was a body.

"Louisa is so artistic," Sam said with obvious pride. "Come on, we'd better take it down."

It didn't take the friends long to dismantle the dummy and soon they were laughing as they made their way back to the spa. As they got there Lola could see Linc waiting for them and a little spark of joy went through her.

"We'll leave you to it," Louisa said and dragged Sam away from them.

"Hi," Linc said. "Do you want to take a walk, or have a coffee or something?"

"I feel like I've been drinking all day, let's take that walk."

He held out his arm and Lola took it and they strolled across the grass and around the corner to the Zen Garden. It was shaded and relaxing there and Linc made his way to the stone benches and indicated for them to sit.

"The police have gone, you were a big help," he said.

Lola nodded, for some reason her throat was dry and she couldn't seem to speak.

"I wondered if my past had put you off, if not, maybe, I could take your number. I would love to call you sometime."

Lola smiled. "I would like that."

"You live at South-Brooke?"

"I do."

"There's a lovely garden center not far from there, Lakeside. Would you meet me there for a coffee next week? Sassy can come too."

Lola was surprised that she wanted to see him again. Her luck with men had not been good but maybe it was time to give romance one more try.

"We'd love to."

"I see you, but will expect sausage," Sassy grumbled at Linc while tapping his leg with her paw."

"I think she likes the idea," Linc said.

"You might have to bribe her but you have won her over."

"Well, that's just made my day, come here, pooch." Linc picked Sassy up and fed her another piece of dog chocolate. It seemed he had an endless supply.

OH OH

THREE WEEKS LATER.

Alice, Tilly, Lola, and Sassy were spending the day at the prestigious Woofs dog show. Sitting on the benches around the main arena they were killing time waiting for Alice's friend to join them.

"That didn't seem like the right decision, well, to me," Tilly said and Lola tended to agree. "I don't know much about dogs and showing, but the one that won... I would have put it last."

"I would agree with you," Lola said.

Alice let out a sigh. Her friend, Una Freeman, was a renowned judge and had just awarded the famous Woof's Best in Show to a rather portly Labrador. It had been such a shock result that a howl of dismay had gone up throughout the arena. Mark Duncan, who was the favorite with his honey-colored miniature poodle, Fifi, had actually walked out of the arena, forfeiting his second place.

"It wasn't a decision I expected Una to make. She's normally very fair," Alice said. "I wonder where she can be, she's usually very prompt."

Sassy crawled across the space between Lola and passed Tilly to Alice. Once there she rolled onto her back waiting for a belly rub.

"Look at you, so cute." Alice leaned over to oblige pushing back the purple sleeve of her shell suit. It was a bright lavender with a big yellow stripe across the middle. "You would have won the prize for your cheek."

"Cheeks pretty," Sassy said smiling even wider.

"Maybe we should go and see where she is?" Tilly asked.

"Has it been that long?" Alice checked her watch. "Oh, my, she's an hour late, something must be wrong."

"Let's go see if we can find her." Lola stood and picked up her rucksack. It had been a fun morning but she was ready for some lunch.

"Of course." Alice led the way and weaved through the crowds past the rings and the benches where all the show dogs were kept in between their performances. "The room she was using is just at the end of this hall," Alice said.

As they got closer Sassy dropped her nose to the ground and began sniffing. "What is it?" Lola asked.

"Nasty plant." Sassy carried on sniffing and was pulling on her lead.

Lola wanted to tell her that if it was so nasty, that she should probably stop sniffing it but she knew that wouldn't work and it was a hard conversation to have, surreptitiously.

"Here we go." Alice knocked on a green door and waited for an answer. There was none. "Maybe she went to look for us." Alice shook her head. "She's not normally like this."

"Call her again," Tilly said.

Alice pulled her phone from her shell suit pocket. "She's not looked at the last message yet."

"Go on, call her." Tilly shrugged.

"Oh, oh," Sassy said and pawed on the door of the room.

Lola had a sinking feeling. Whatever was making Sassy worried was behind that door and it was, no doubt, the reason why Una had not met them for lunch."

Alice was holding her mobile phone, as the British called a cell, to her ear and shaking her head. "She's not answering."

Lola walked up to the door and tried the handle. It turned and as it did she wished that she had covered the handle first. If this ended up being a crime scene she had just smudged any prints that might have been on that handle.

Lola pushed open the door and the scene inside took her breath away. A worried-looking dalmatian dog was curled up on the floor next to the body of Una. The floor of the small room was covered in what looked like bloody pawprints.

There had been a death at the dog show, now Lola had to find out if it was murder or if the dog had somehow caused an accident.

"Oh, my, Una!" Alice said as she rushed into the room.

You can now grab the first 6 Bulldog on the Case books in one great value box set and also FREE with Kindle Unlimited

Or Grab the next book here

RED WINE, MUSTARD, AND MINT LAMB SHANKS SLOW COOKER RECIPE

Serves 4

4 lamb shanks

2 tbsp olive oil

1/2 tsp salt and pepper

2 medium, onions finely chopped

4, garlic cloves crushed

1 cup of red wine

2 cups of beef stock

2 tbsp Worcestershire sauce

2 tbsp whole grain mustard

2 tbsp honey

1 handful of mint leaves, roughly chopped

500g baby carrots

Seasonal greens

Set your slow cooker to low.

Heat a frying pan to moderate-high heat and add half the olive oil.

Season the lamb with salt and pepper and brown in the pan, turning often. Once browned set it to one side.

To make the sauce:

Add the remaining oil to the frying pan and add the chopped onions and garlic, stirring for about 15 seconds, or until fragrant.

Add the wine, bring to the boil and boil for 1 minute.

Add the beef stock, Worcestershire sauce, mustard, honey, and half the chopped mint

and bring to a gentle simmer then remove from the heat.

Transfer the lamb to the slow cooker and pour the sauce over it.

Cover and cook on low for 8 hours or high for approx. 4 hours, or until the meat is tender and easily pulled from the bone.

Approx 2 hours before the end of cooking add the baby carrots and stir through the sauce.

Serve with mashed Kumara and seasonal vegetables.

KUMARA

Kumara is often referred to as a sweet potato, but it belongs to the morning glory (Convolvulaceae) family, and not, like potato, to the nightshade one (Solanaceae). And it is not a yam! (Yams belong to the lily or Dioscoreaceae family.) The modern kumara plant is a climbing vine, with tubers and is a very nice accompaniment to a meal.

DOG CHOCOLATES RECIPE

Chocolate is extremely toxic for cats and dogs. Luckily, carob, a sweet fruit that looks like a brown pea pod has been used as a chocolate substitute for decades.

Carob contains twice the amount of calcium as Cocoa and is fat-free. It has been used to treat diarrhea in dogs and cats and is known to improve digestion and lower cholesterol.

Once made keep in the fridge for up to 2 weeks.

Ingredients

- 3/4 cup Unsweetened Carob Powder

- 1/2 cup Frozen Blueberries, unthawed
- 1 cup Unrefined Organic Coconut Oil
- 2 tsp Pure Vanilla Extract

Directions

1. Microwave coconut oil for 10-15 seconds or until melted.
2. Combine carob powder, vanilla extract, and coconut oil in a large mixing bowl, and whisk together.
3. Fold in the unthawed blueberries and set them aside.
4. Pour the carob mixture into a silicone candy bar mold.
5. Place the mold into the freezer for 30 minutes.
6. Set out for 5 minutes and serve.

ALSO BY ROSIE SAMS

To be the first to find out when Rosie releases a new book join and to grab occasional free stories join my newsletter

You can now grab the first 6 Bulldog on the Case books in one great value box set and also FREE with Kindle Unlimited.

Follow Rosie Sams on Bookbub

Follow Rosie Sams on Amazon

Printed in Great Britain
by Amazon

85383225R00194